S0-ANO-417

Dear parents, caregivers, and educators:

If you want to get your child excited about reading, you've come to the right place! Ready-to-Read *GRAPHICS* is the perfect launchpad for emerging graphic novel readers.

All Ready-to-Read *GRAPHICS* books include the following:

★ **A how-to guide to reading graphic novels for first-time readers**

★ **Easy-to-follow panels to support reading comprehension**

★ **Accessible vocabulary to build your child's reading confidence**

★ **Compelling stories that star your child's favorite characters**

★ **Fresh, engaging illustrations that provide context and promote visual literacy**

Wherever your child may be on their reading journey, Ready-to-Read *GRAPHICS* will make them giggle, gasp, and want to keep reading more.

Blast off on this starry adventure . . . a universe of graphic novel reading awaits!

CHI-CHI AND PEY-PEY

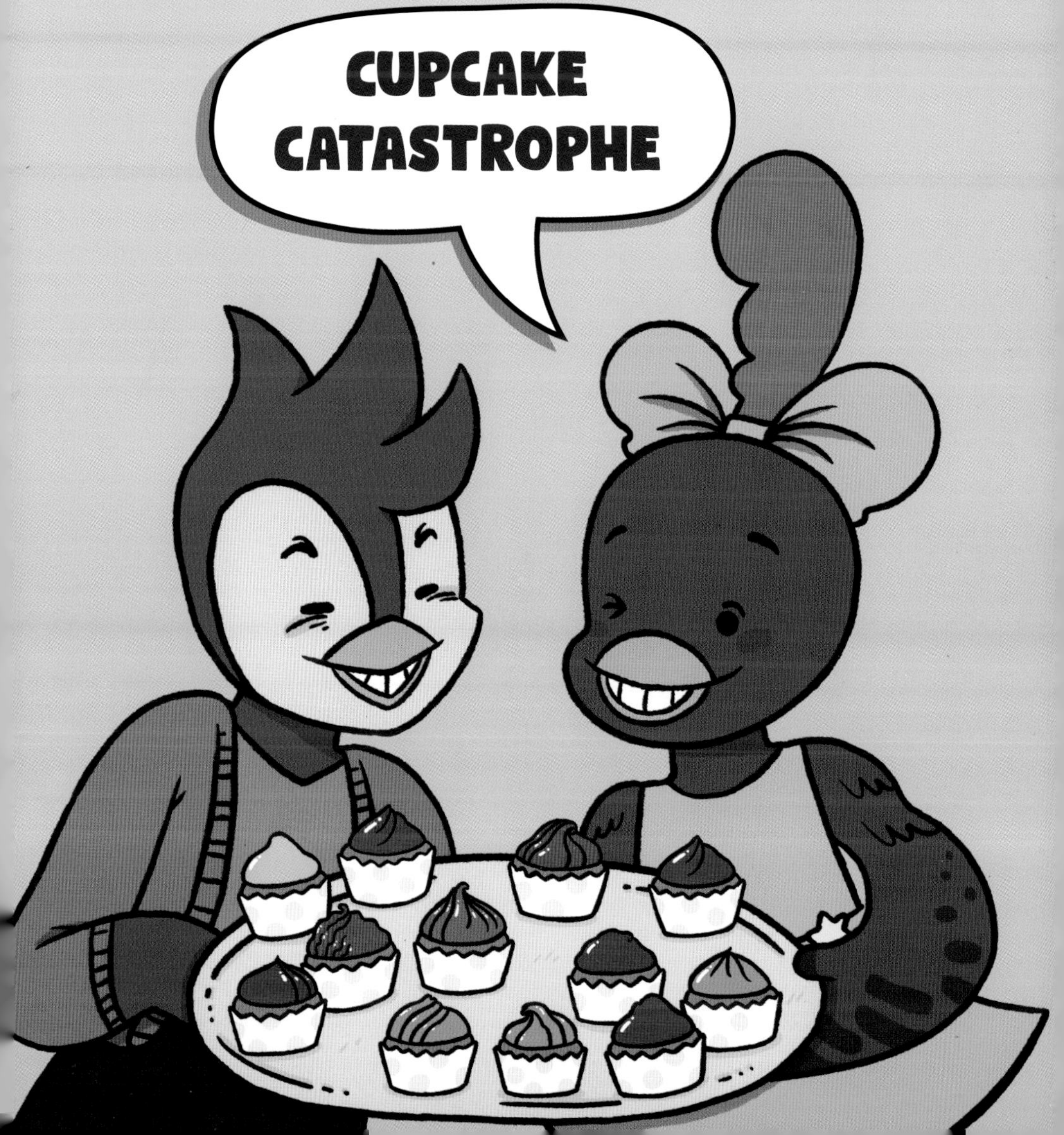
CUPCAKE CATASTROPHE

For the fabulous Deborah, whose most
favorite color is turquoise —J. F.
To my friends —S. P.

SIMON SPOTLIGHT
An imprint of Simon & Schuster Children's Publishing Division
1230 Avenue of the Americas, New York, New York 10020
This Simon Spotlight edition August 2023
Text copyright © 2023 by Jennifer Fosberry
Illustrations copyright © 2023 by Shiho Pate
All rights reserved, including the right of reproduction in whole or in part in
any form. SIMON SPOTLIGHT, READY-TO-READ, and colophon are registered
trademarks of Simon & Schuster, Inc. For information about special discounts
for bulk purchases, please contact Simon & Schuster Special Sales at
1-866-506-1949 or business@simonandschuster.com.
Manufactured in China 0423 SCP
10 9 8 7 6 5 4 3 2 1
Cataloging-in-Publication Data for this title is available from the Library of
Congress.
ISBN 978-1-6659-3201-1 (hc)
ISBN 978-1-6659-3200-4 (pbk)
ISBN 978-1-6659-3202-8 (ebook)

CHi-CHi AND PEY-PEY

CUPCAKE CATASTROPHE

Written by **Jennifer Fosberry**

Illustrated by **Shiho Pate**

Ready-to-Read *GRAPHICS*

Simon Spotlight

New York   London   Toronto   Sydney   New Delhi

HOW TO READ THIS BOOK

Chi-Chi and Pey-Pey are here to give you some tips on reading this book.

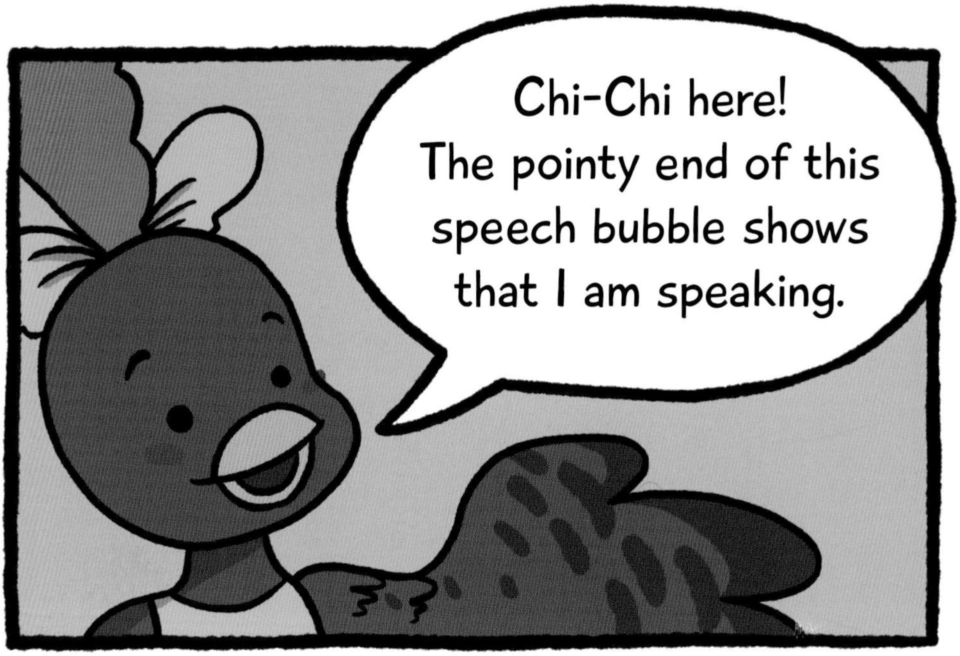
Chi-Chi here!
The pointy end of this speech bubble shows that I am speaking.

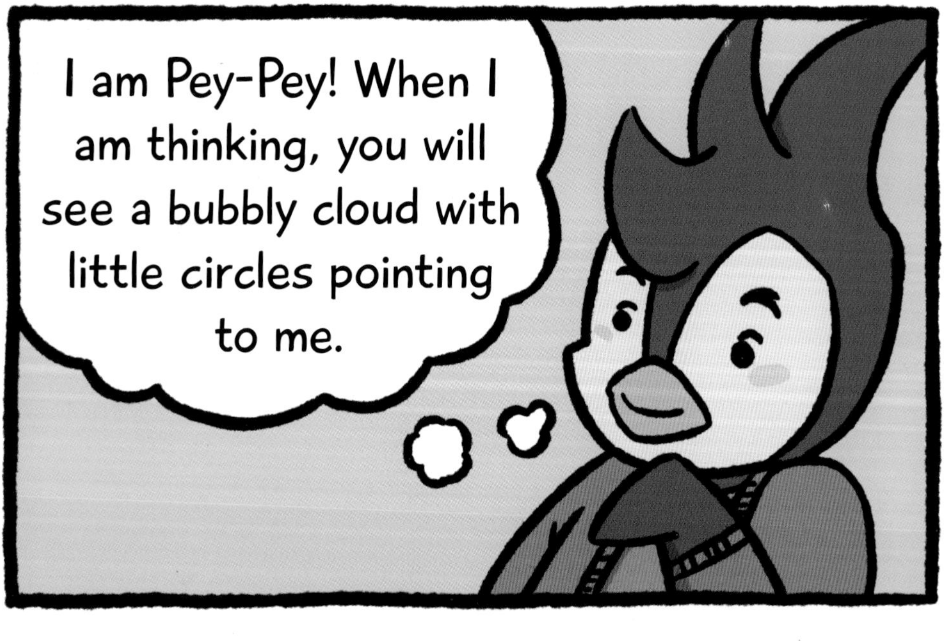
I am Pey-Pey! When I am thinking, you will see a bubbly cloud with little circles pointing to me.

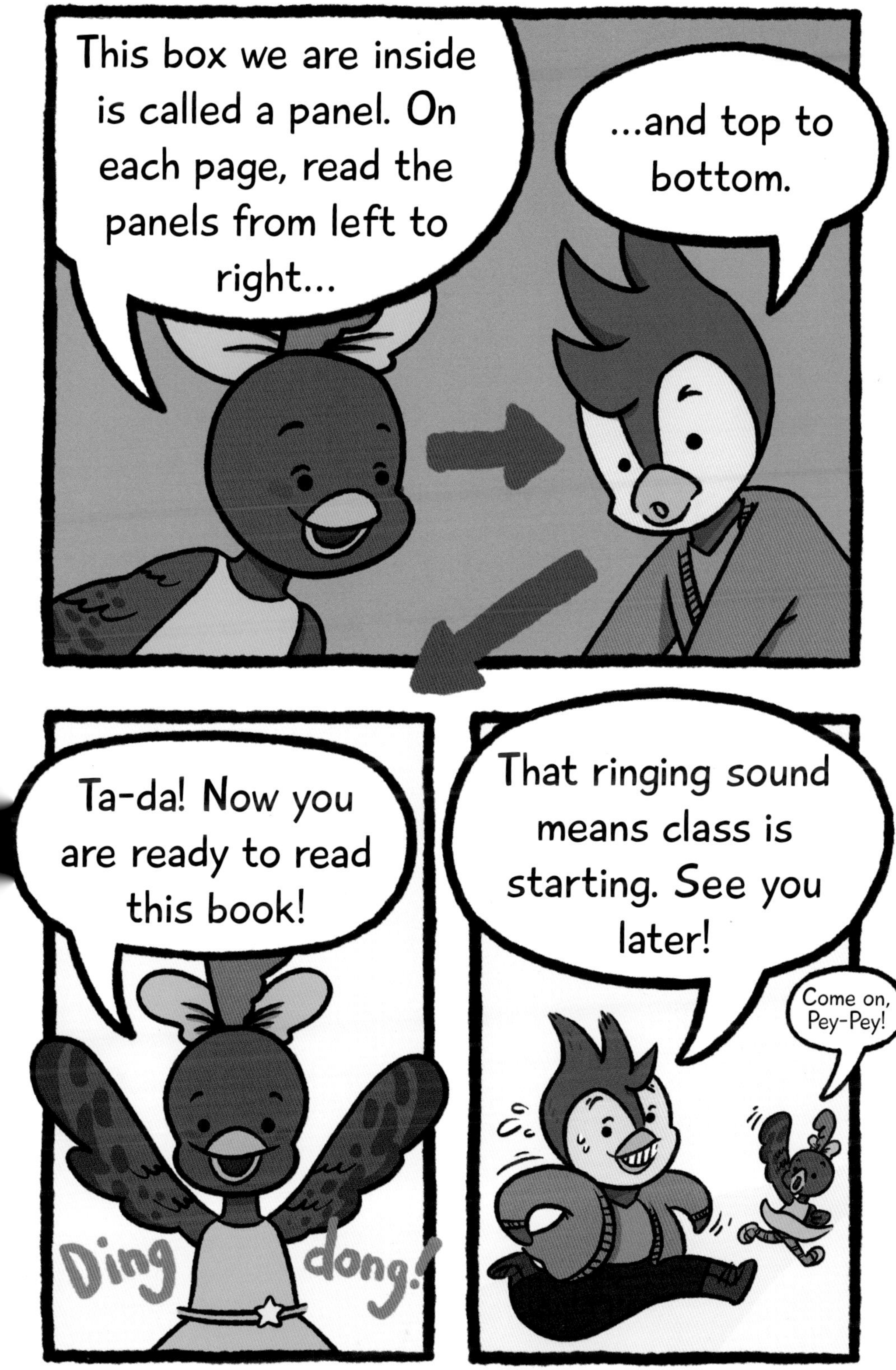
This box we are inside is called a panel. On each page, read the panels from left to right...
...and top to bottom.
Ta-da! Now you are ready to read this book!
Ding dong!
That ringing sound means class is starting. See you later!
Come on, Pey-Pey!

Chi-Chi and Pey-Pey are the very best of friends.

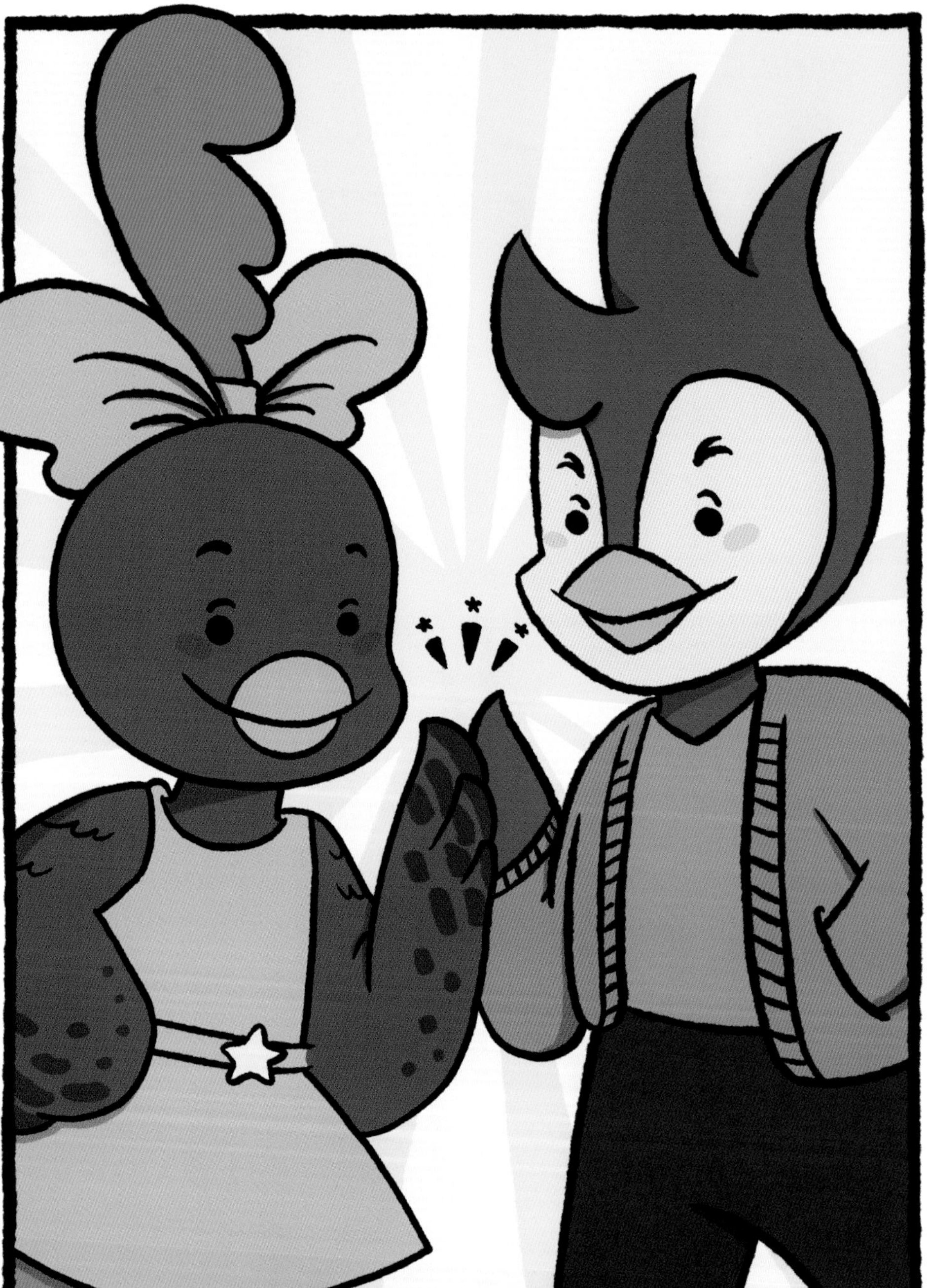

They play together.

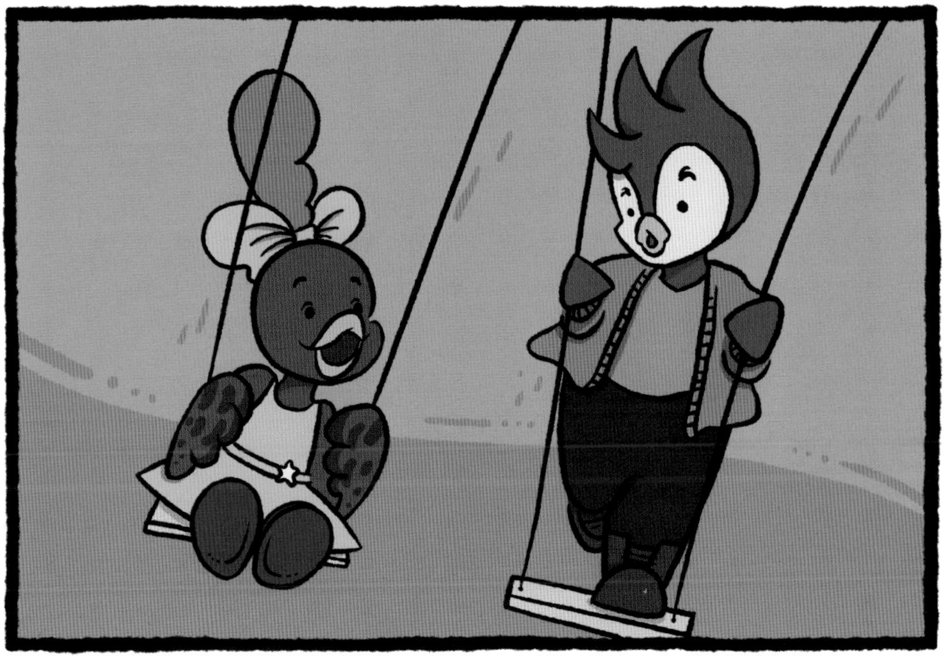

They dance together.

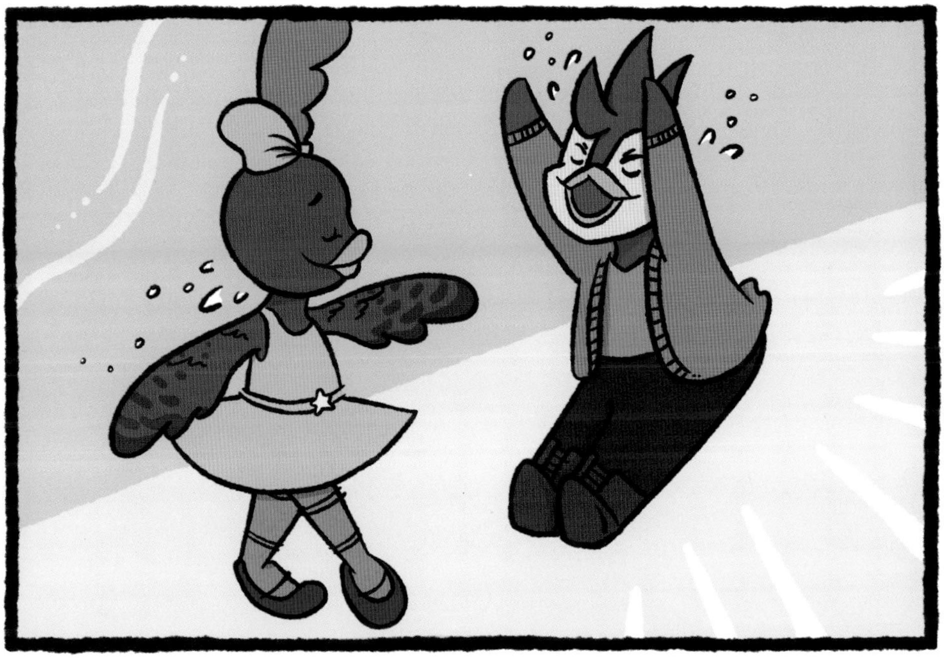

They laugh together.

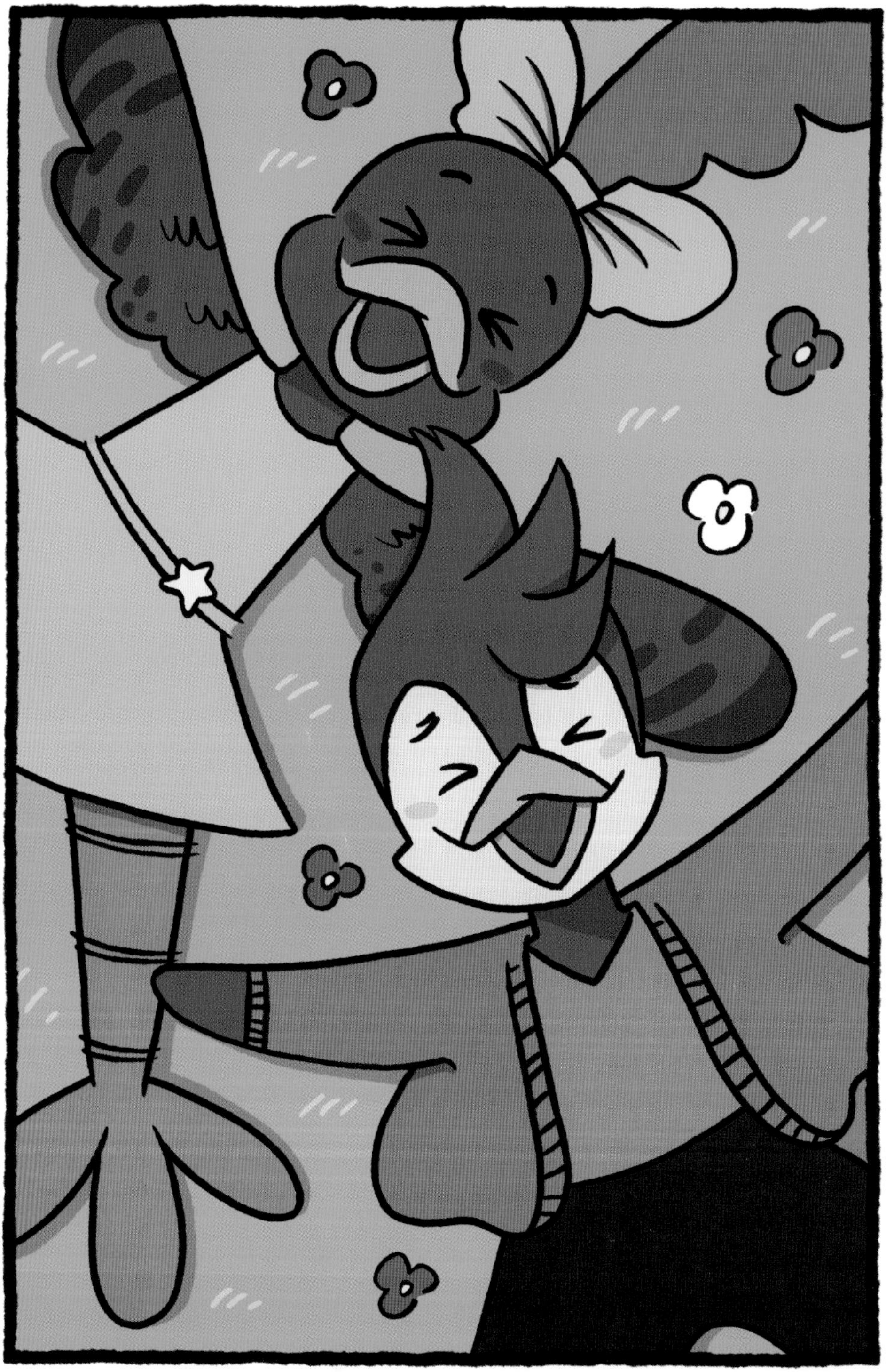

They have fun together at Chi-Chi's house.

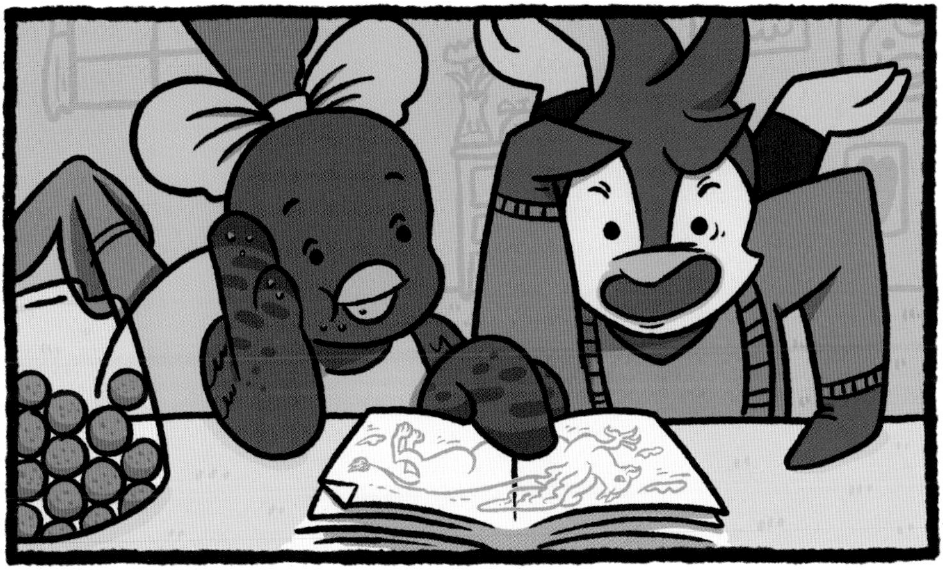

They have fun together at Pey-Pey's house.

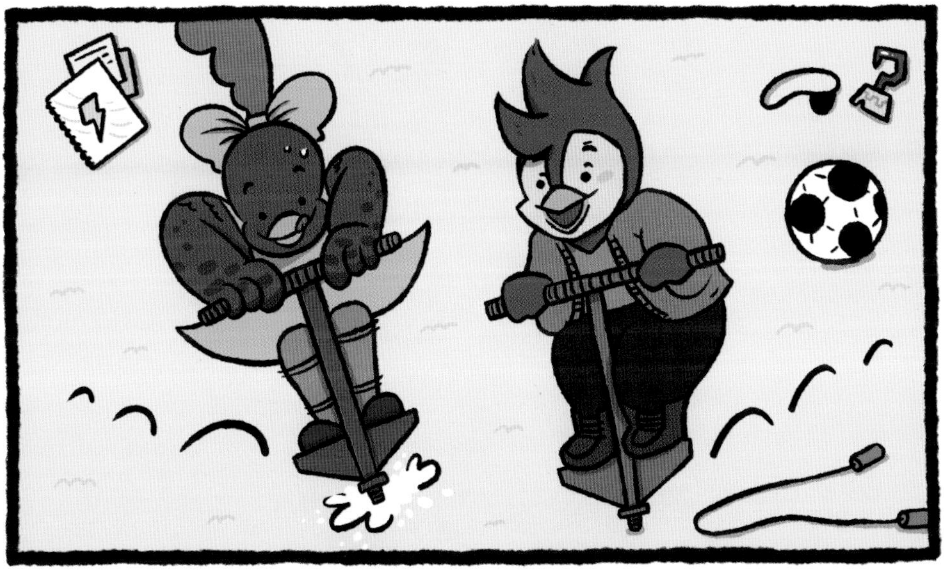

They have fun together at school.

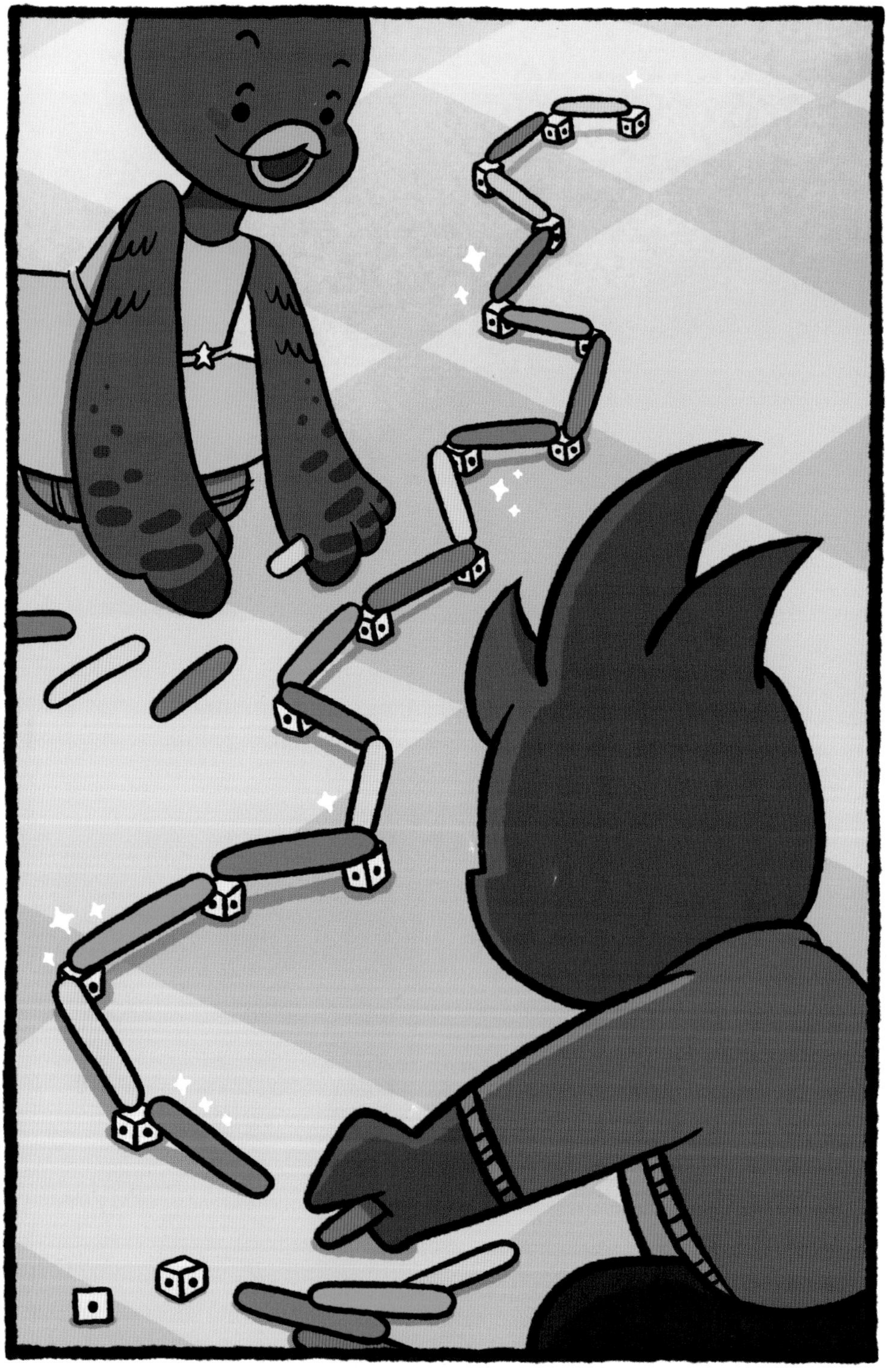

And they never fight.

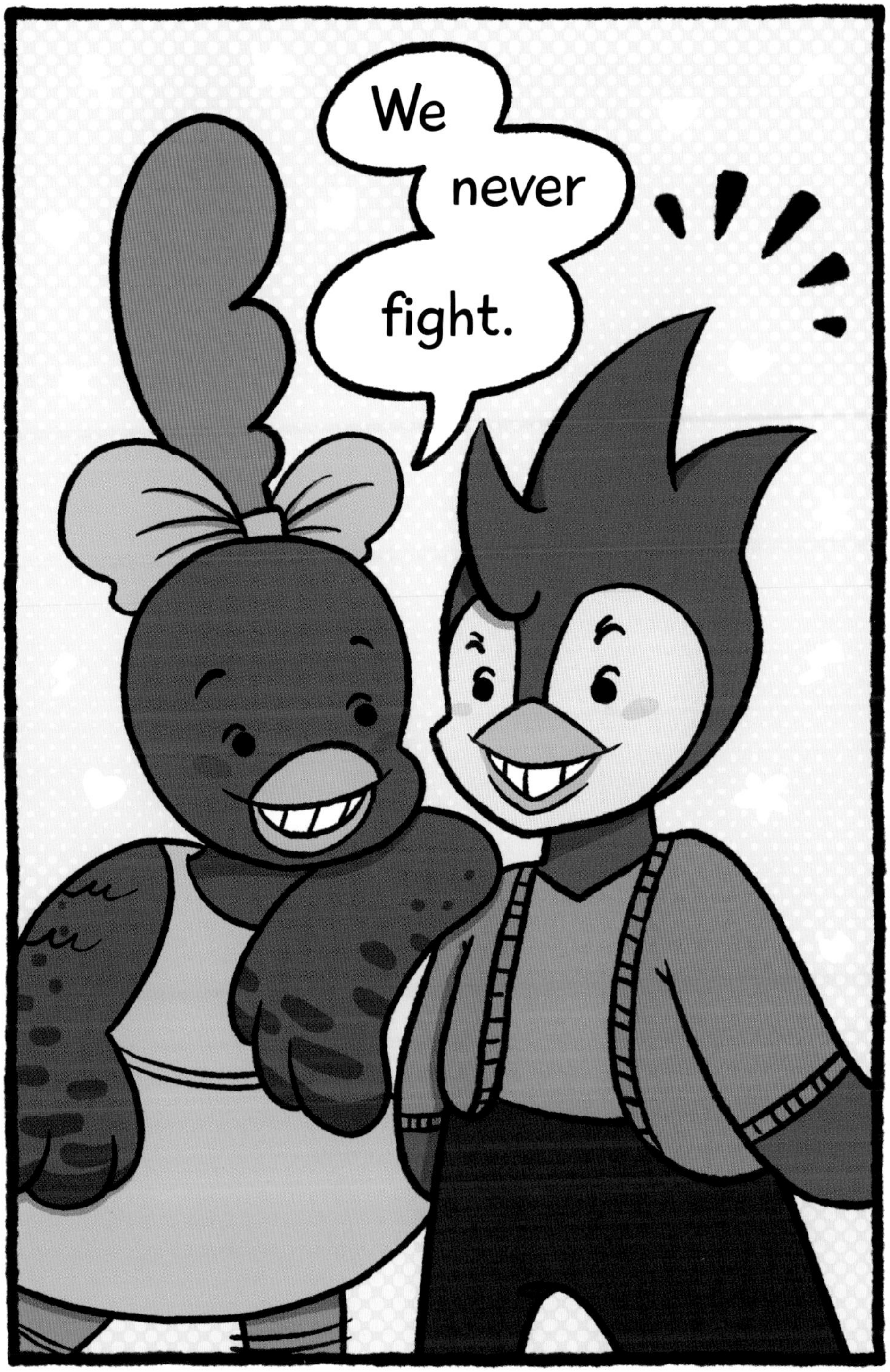
We never fight.

It is art time.

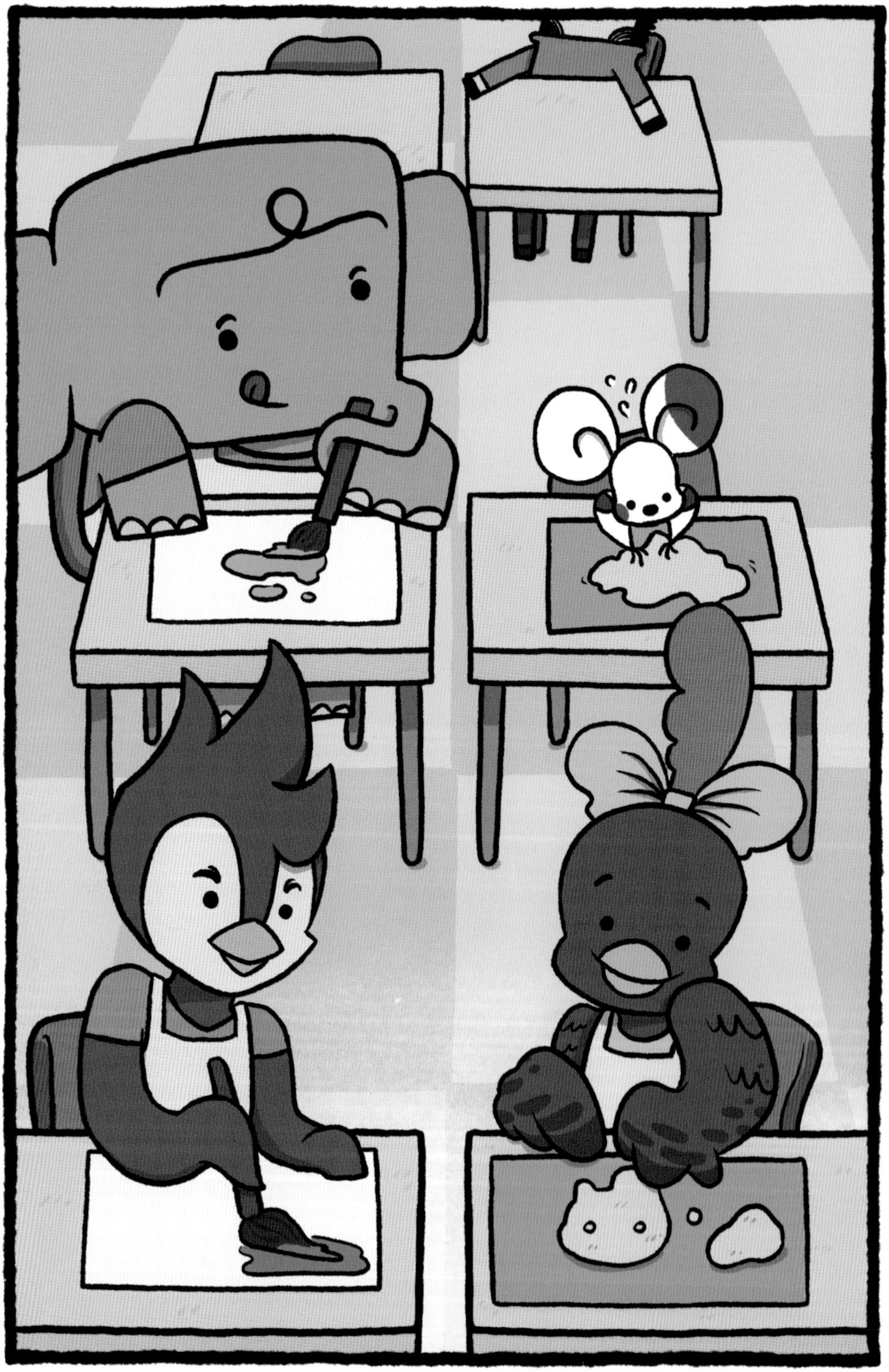

Pey-Pey paints pictures.

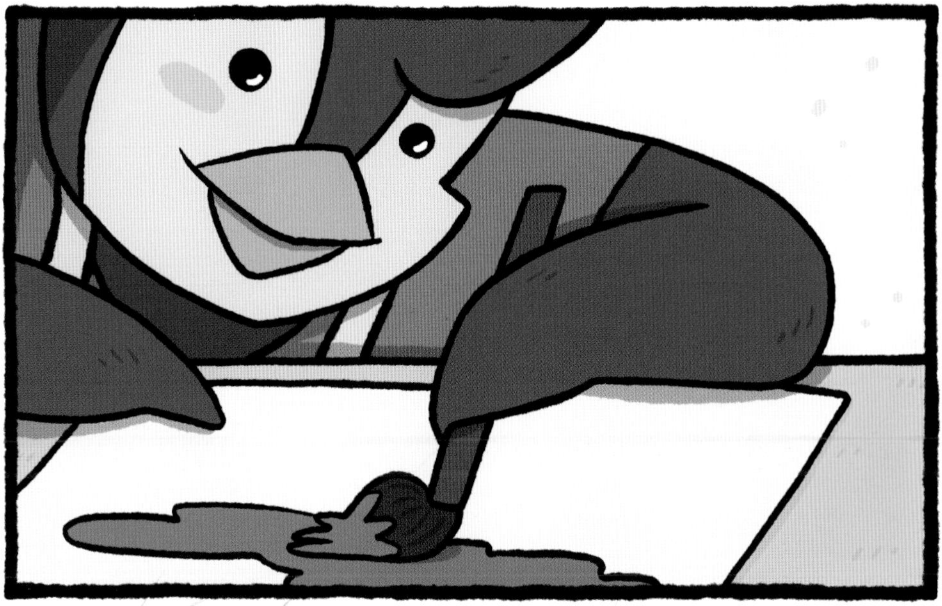

Chi-Chi chooses clay.

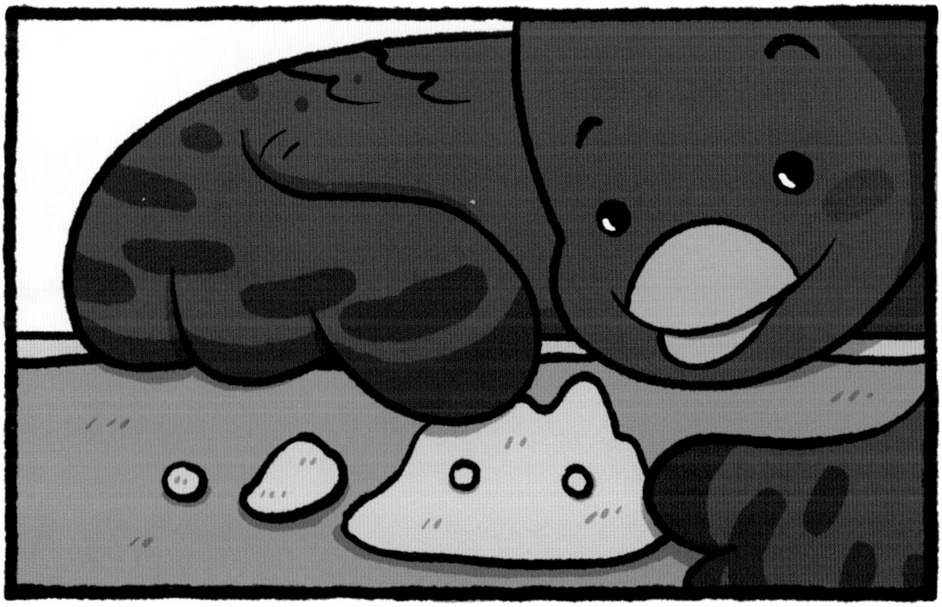

And everyone is happy.

It is music time.

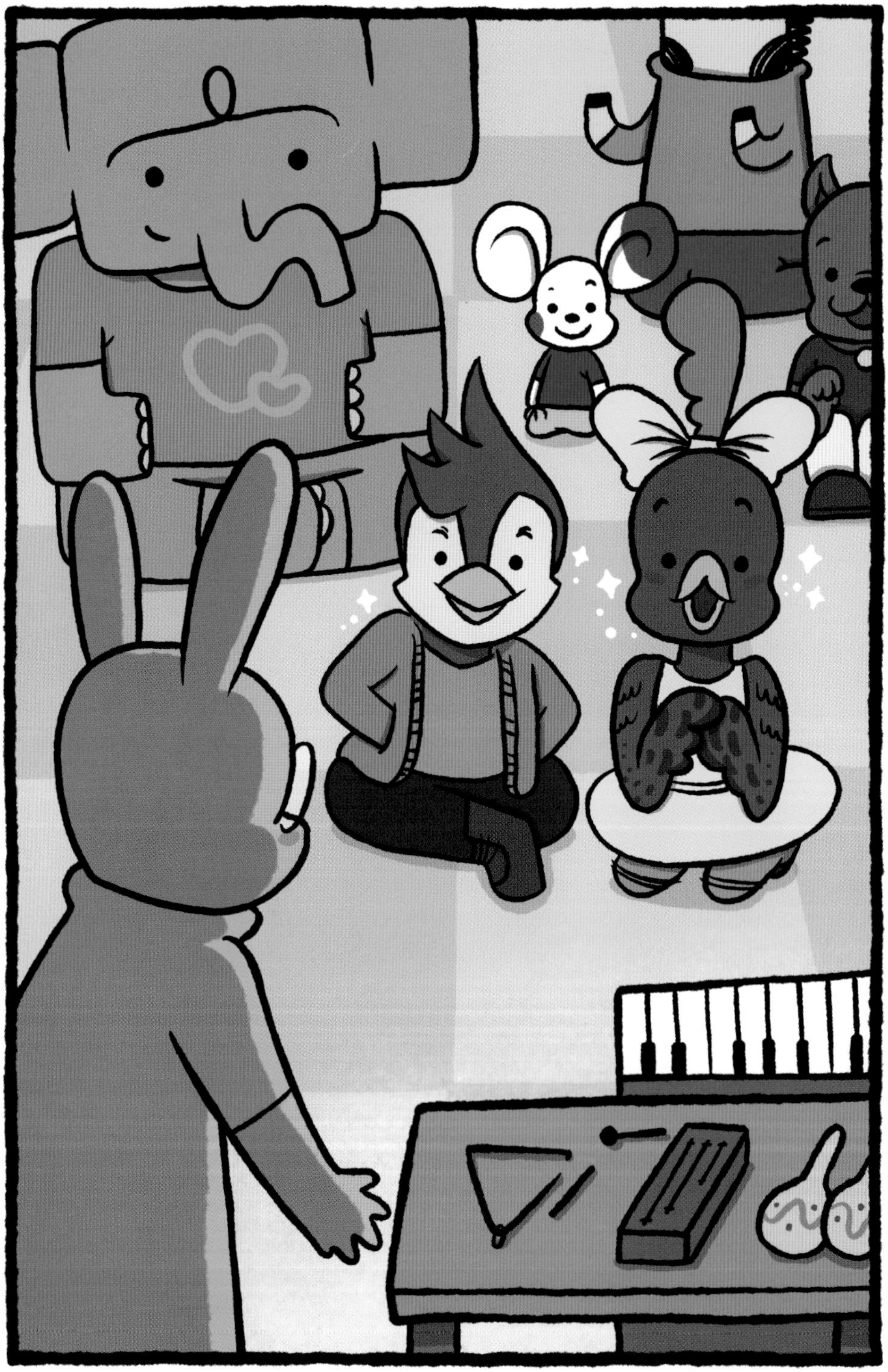

Pey-Pey plays piano.

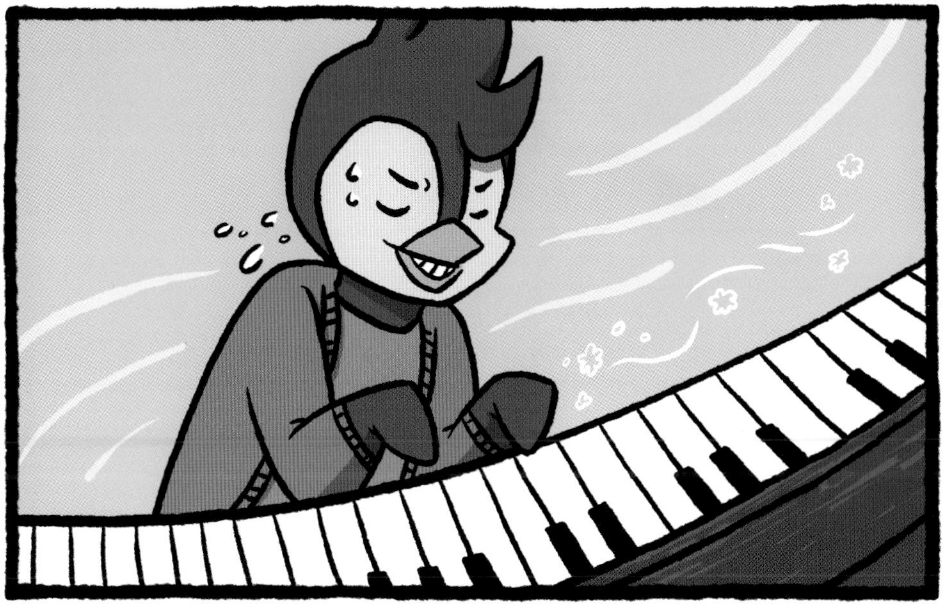

Chi-Chi clinks chimes.

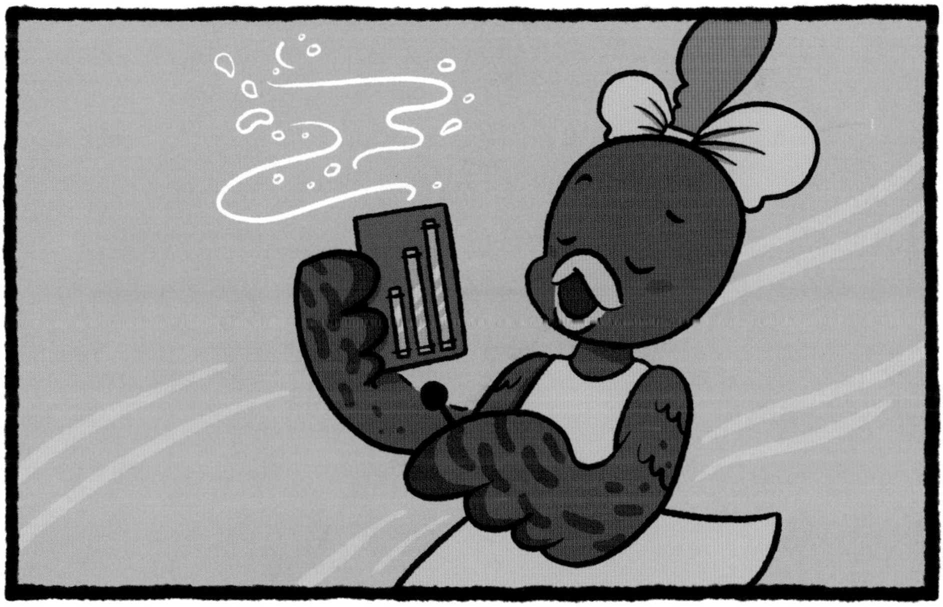

And everyone is happy.

It is snacktime.

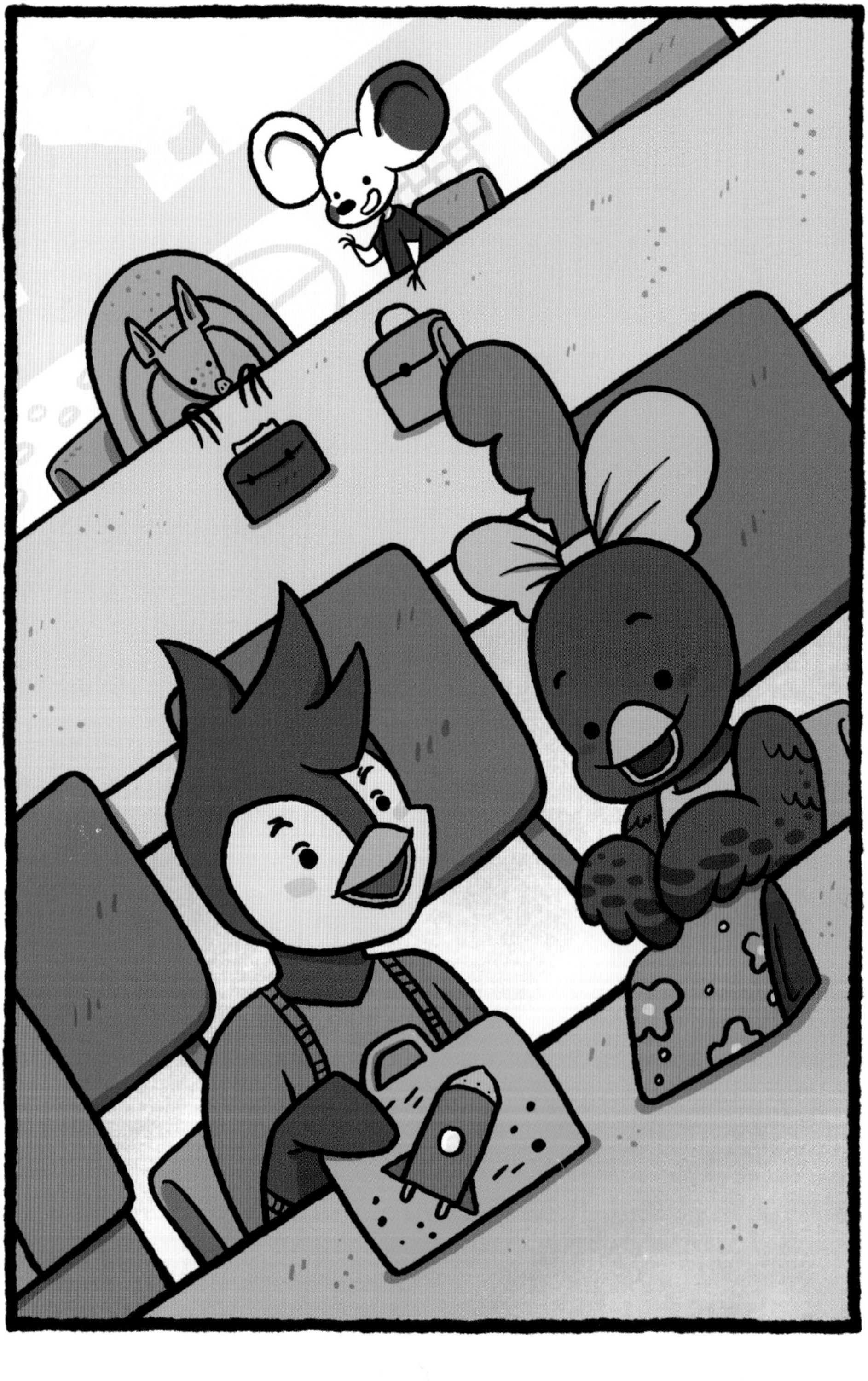

Pey-Pey picks pretzels. Chi-Chi craves crackers.

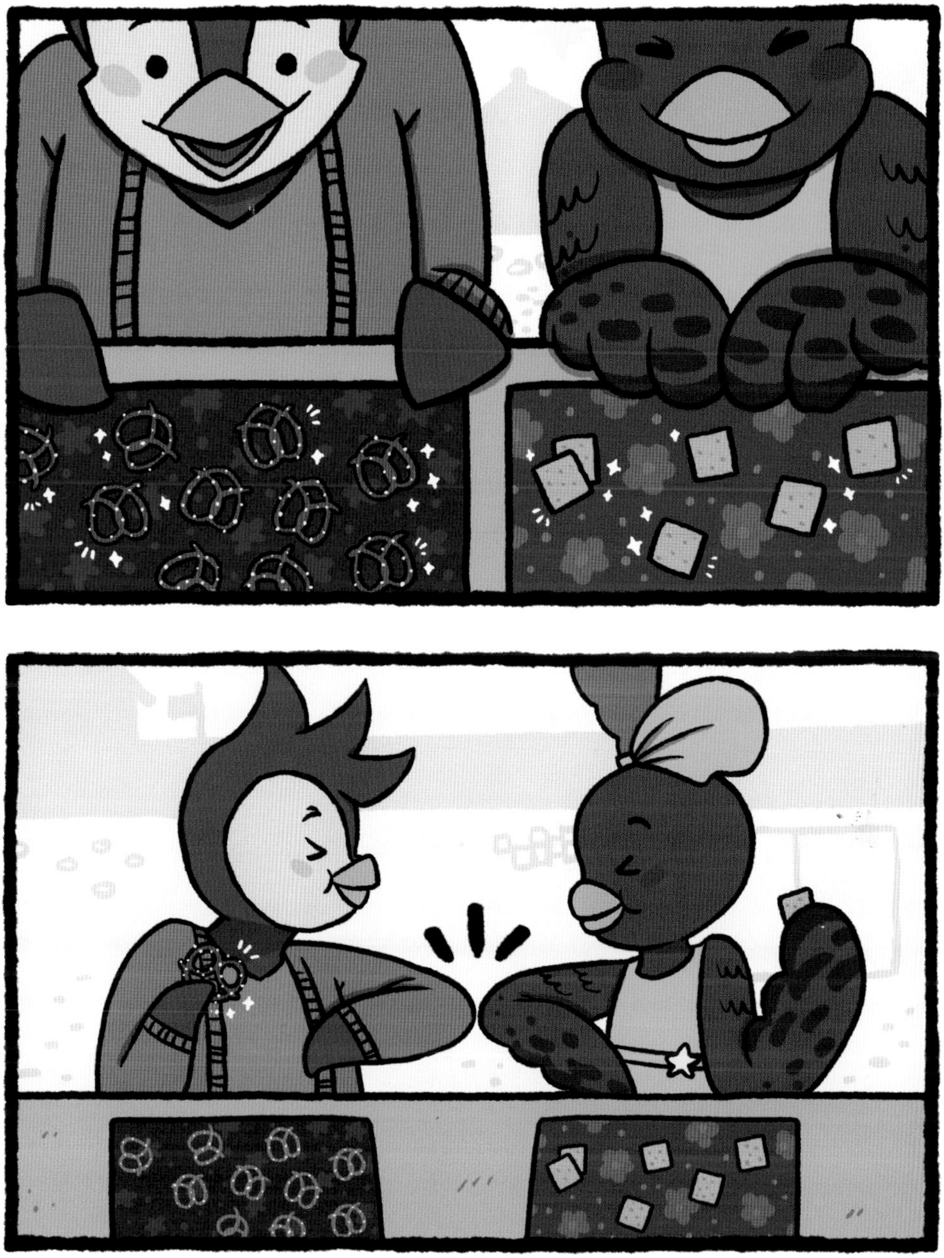

And everyone is happy.

Then there is a bad day at school.

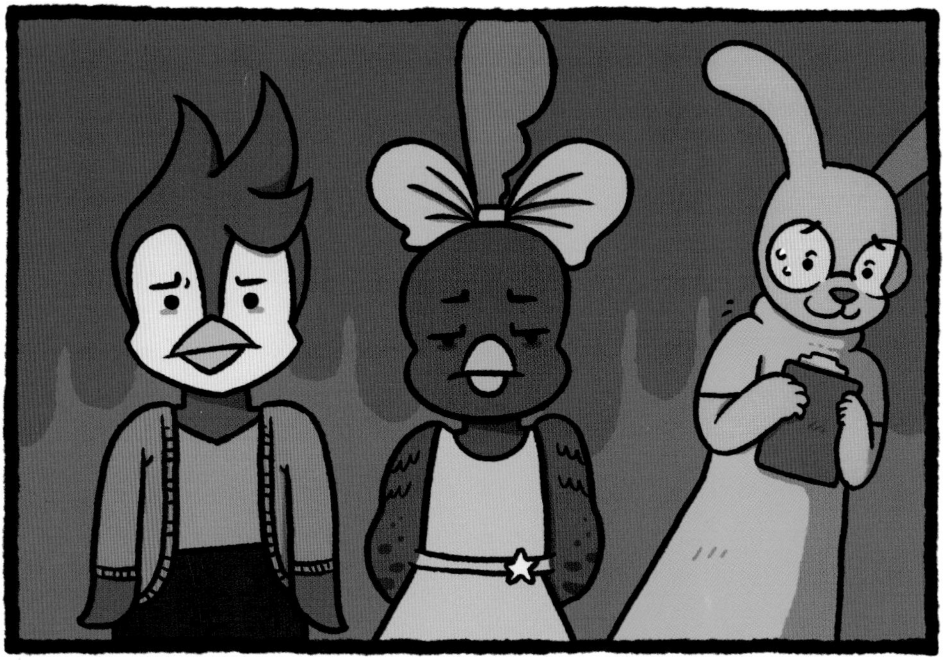

First, the clay is all dried up.

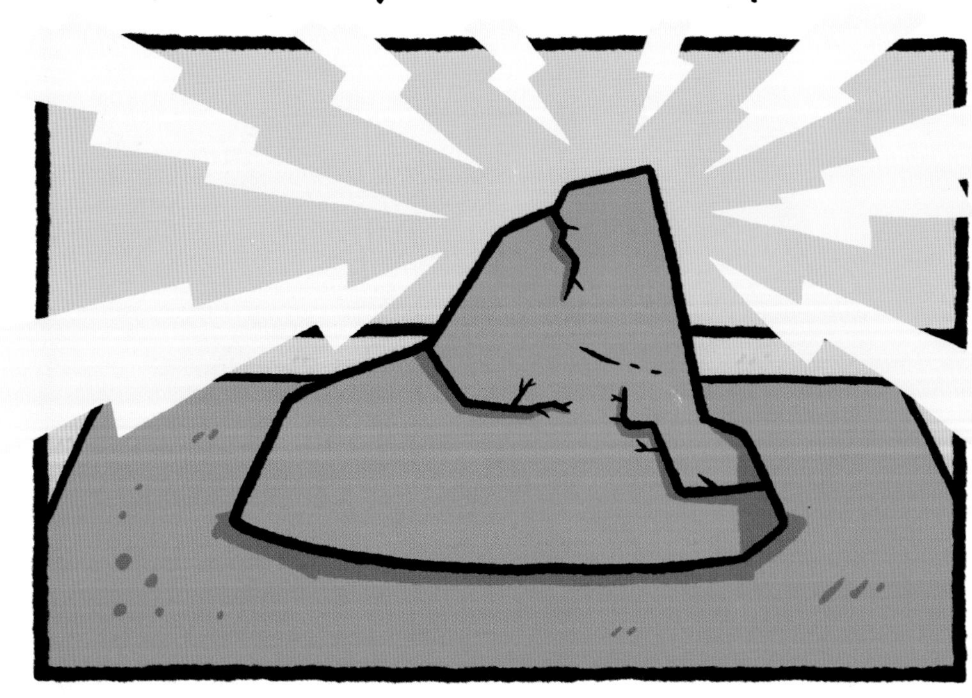

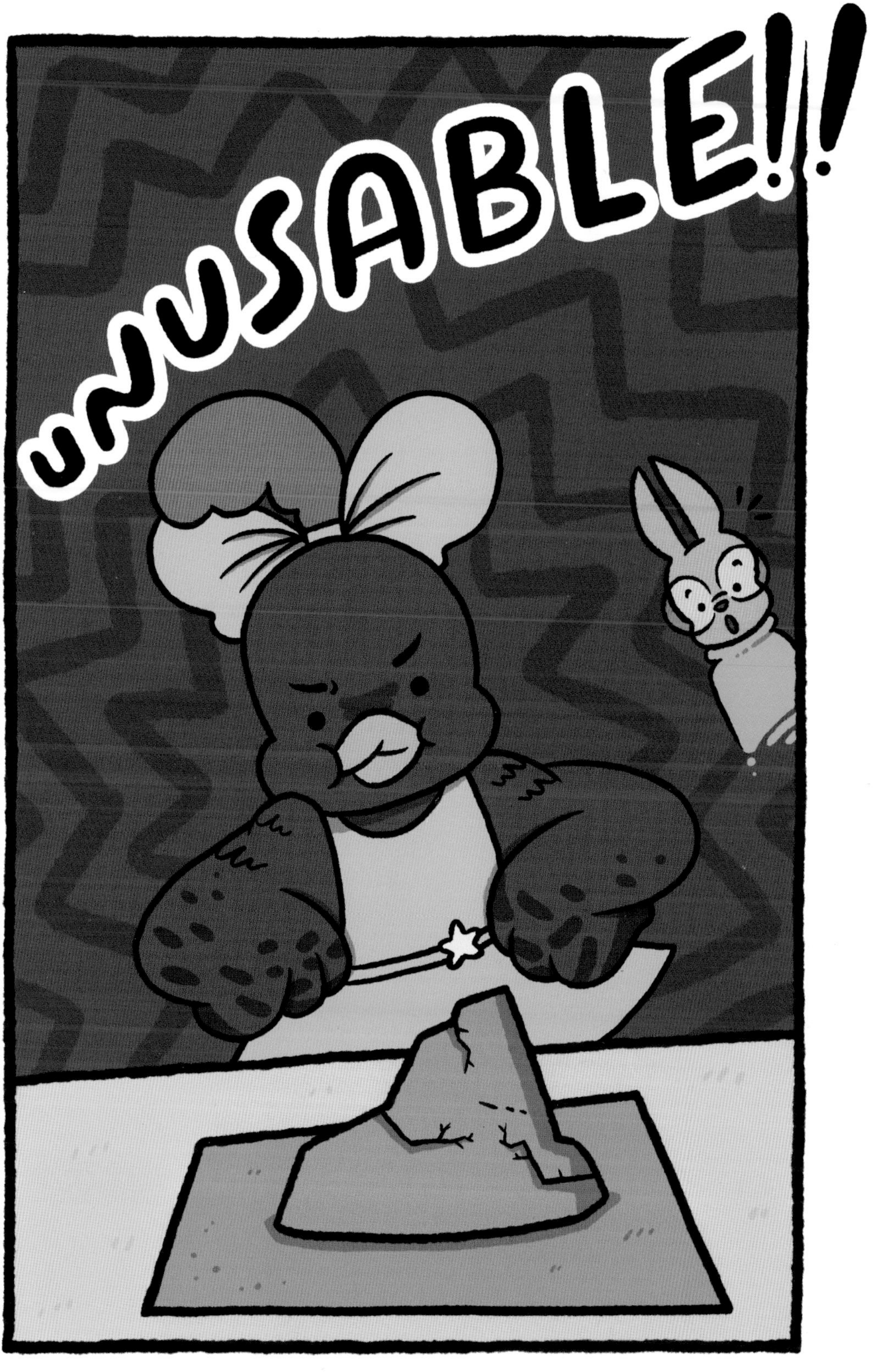
UNUSABLE!!!

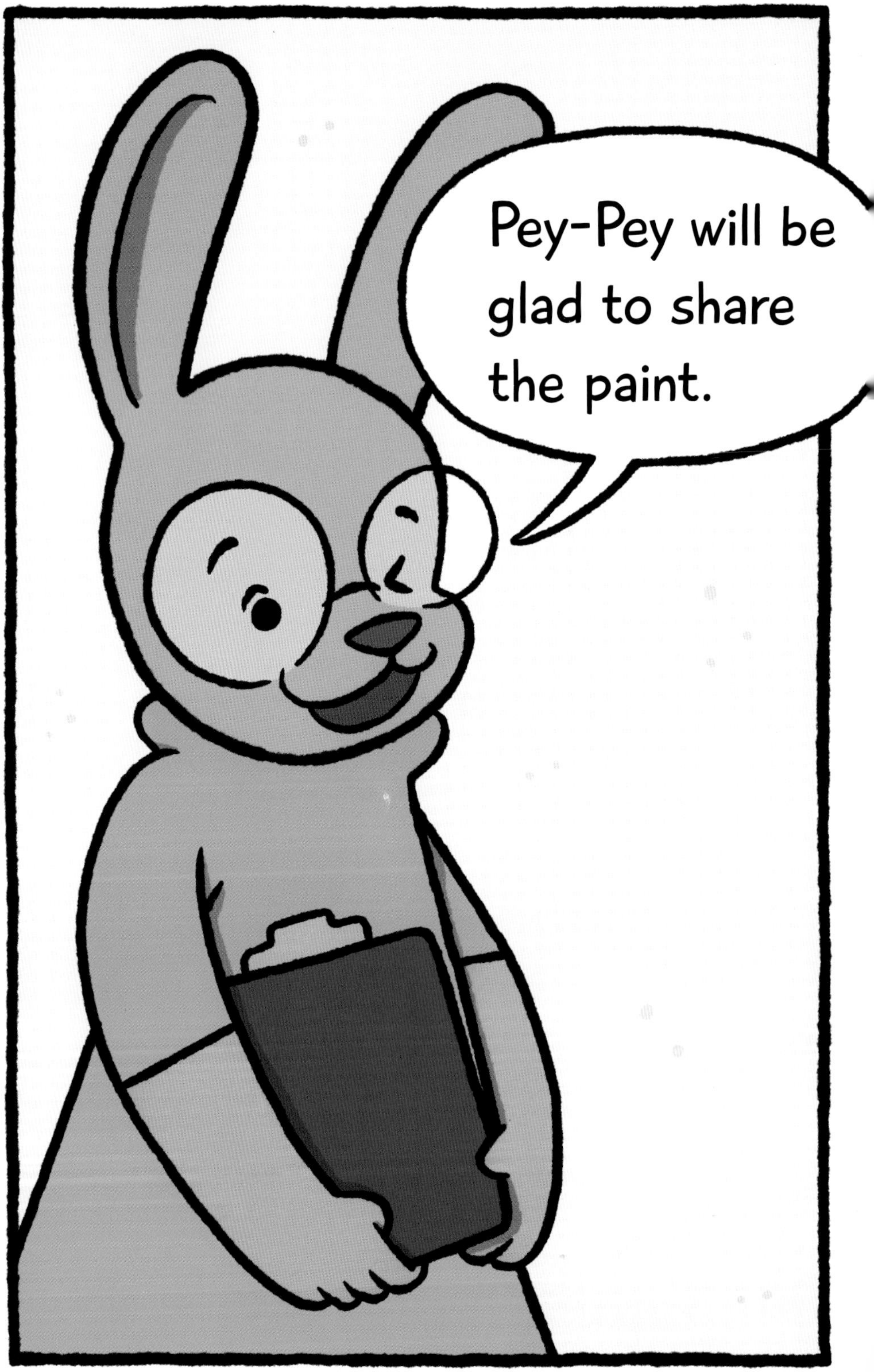
Pey-Pey will be glad to share the paint.

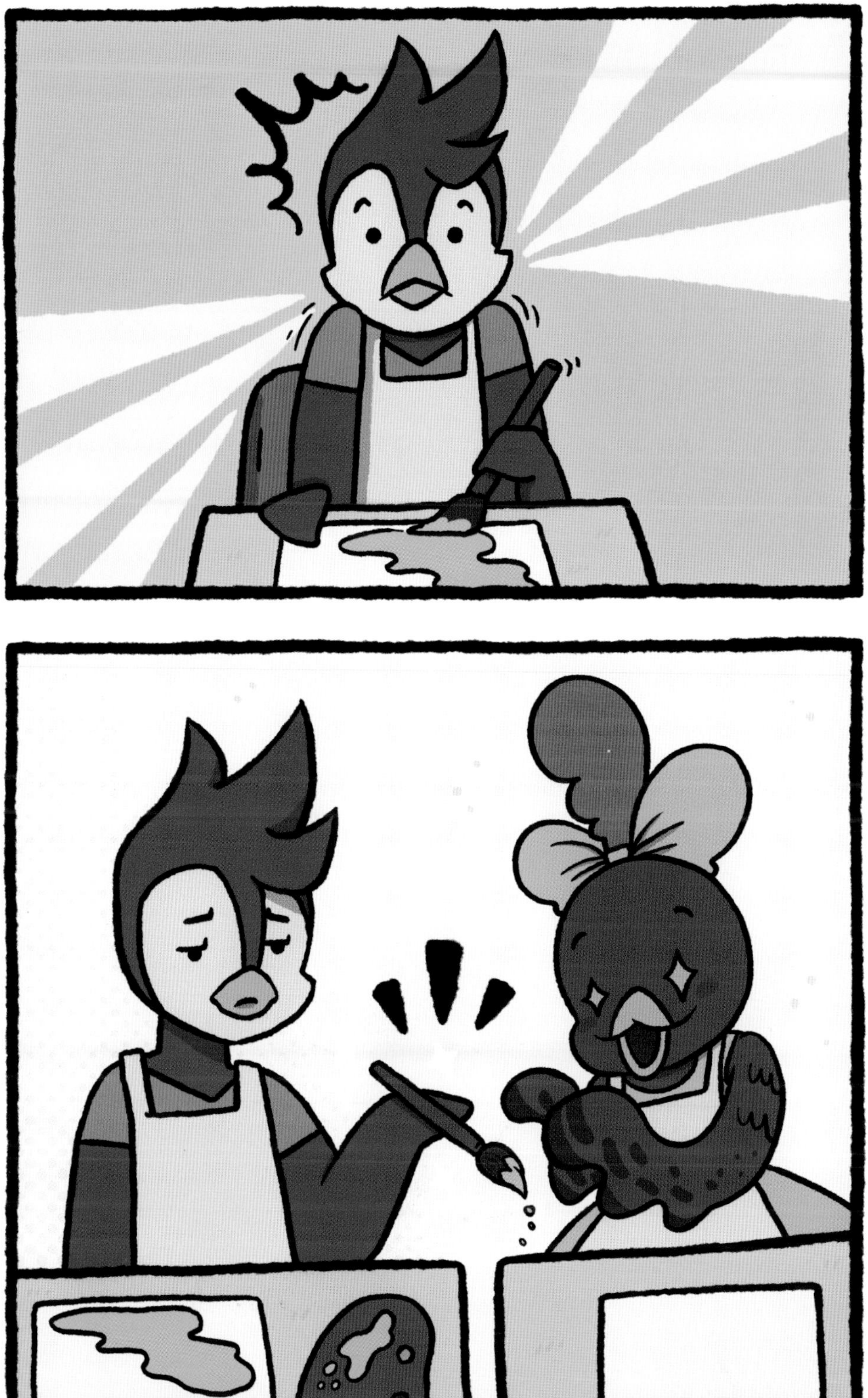

And everyone is happy.

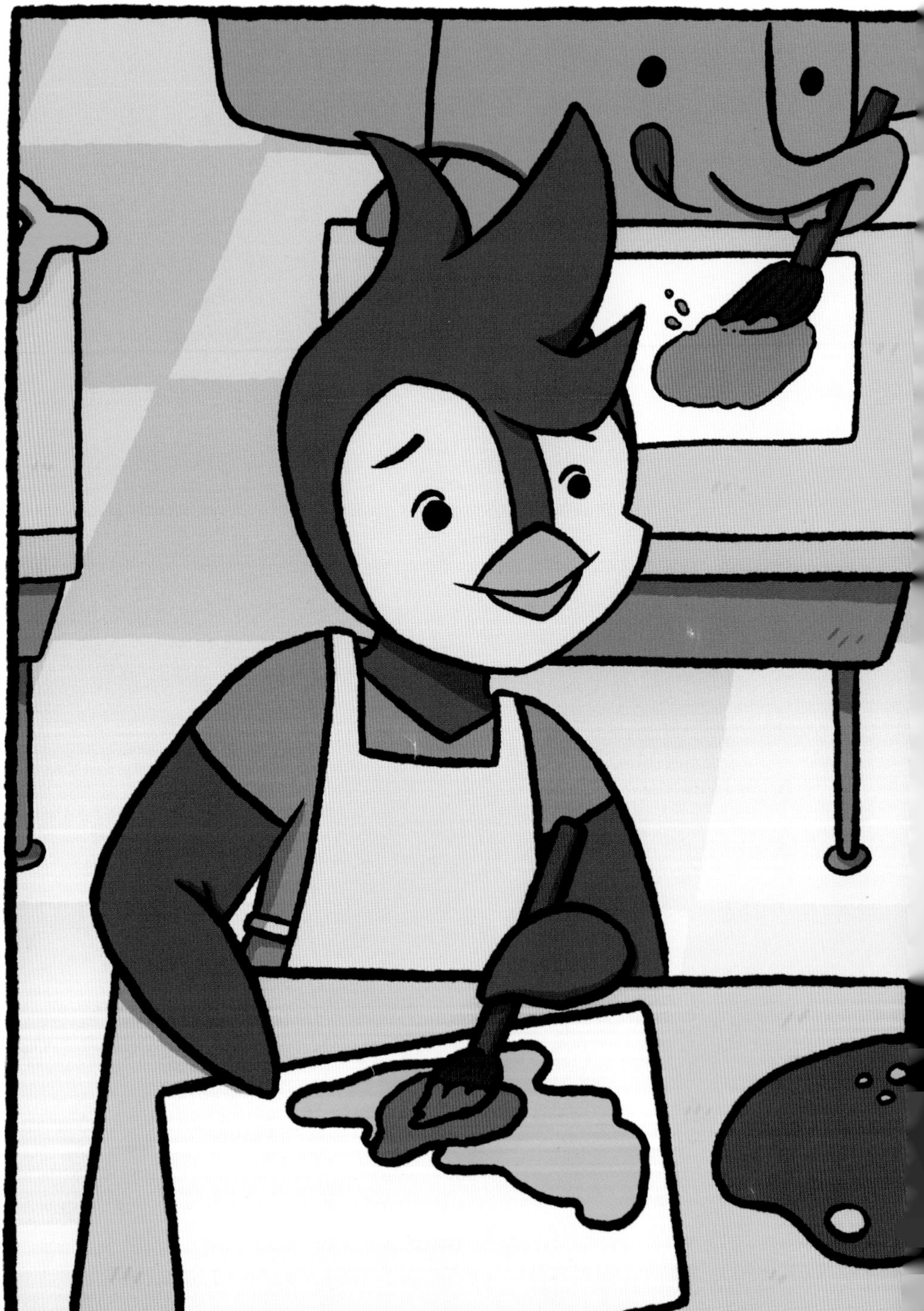

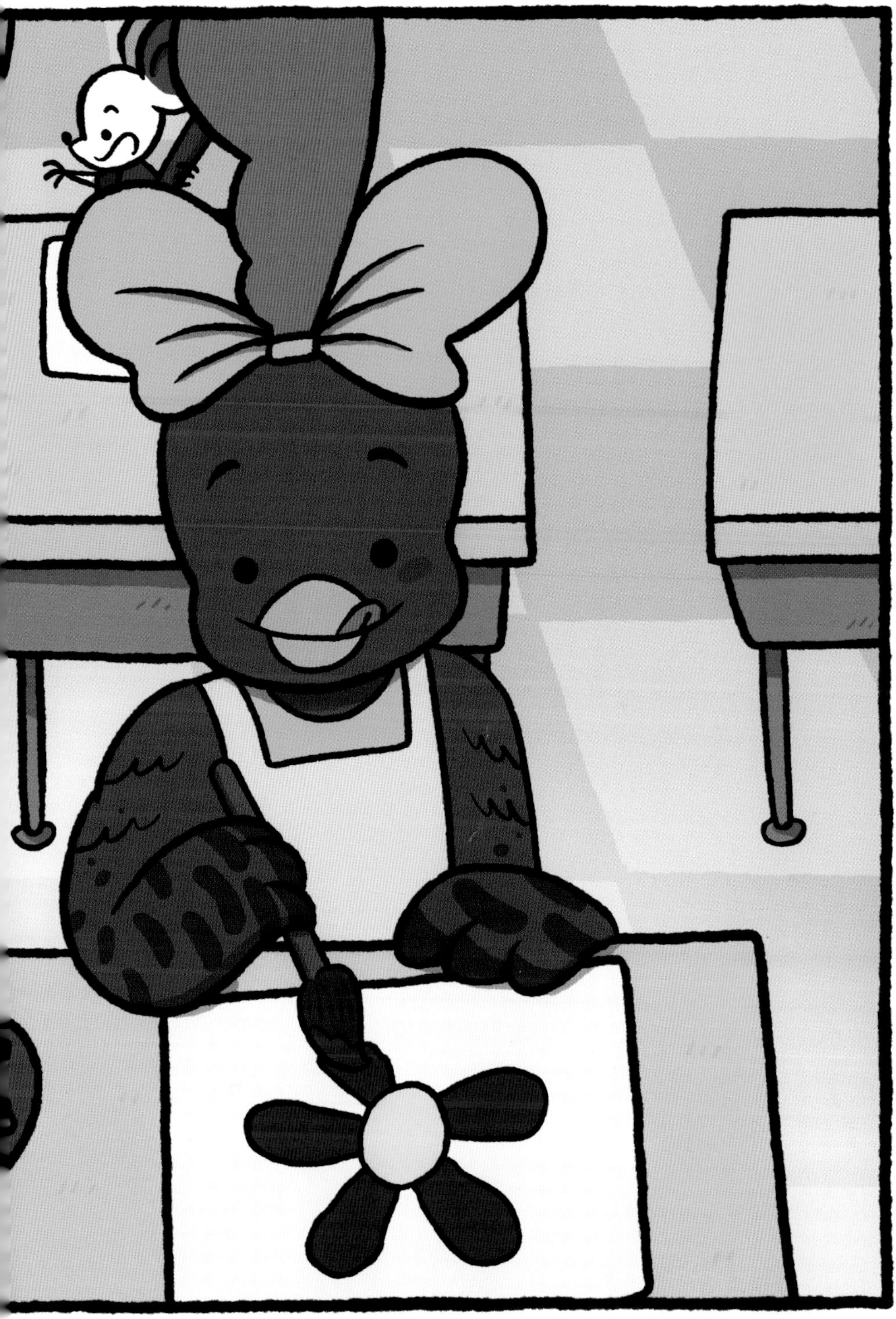

Next, the piano is out of tune.

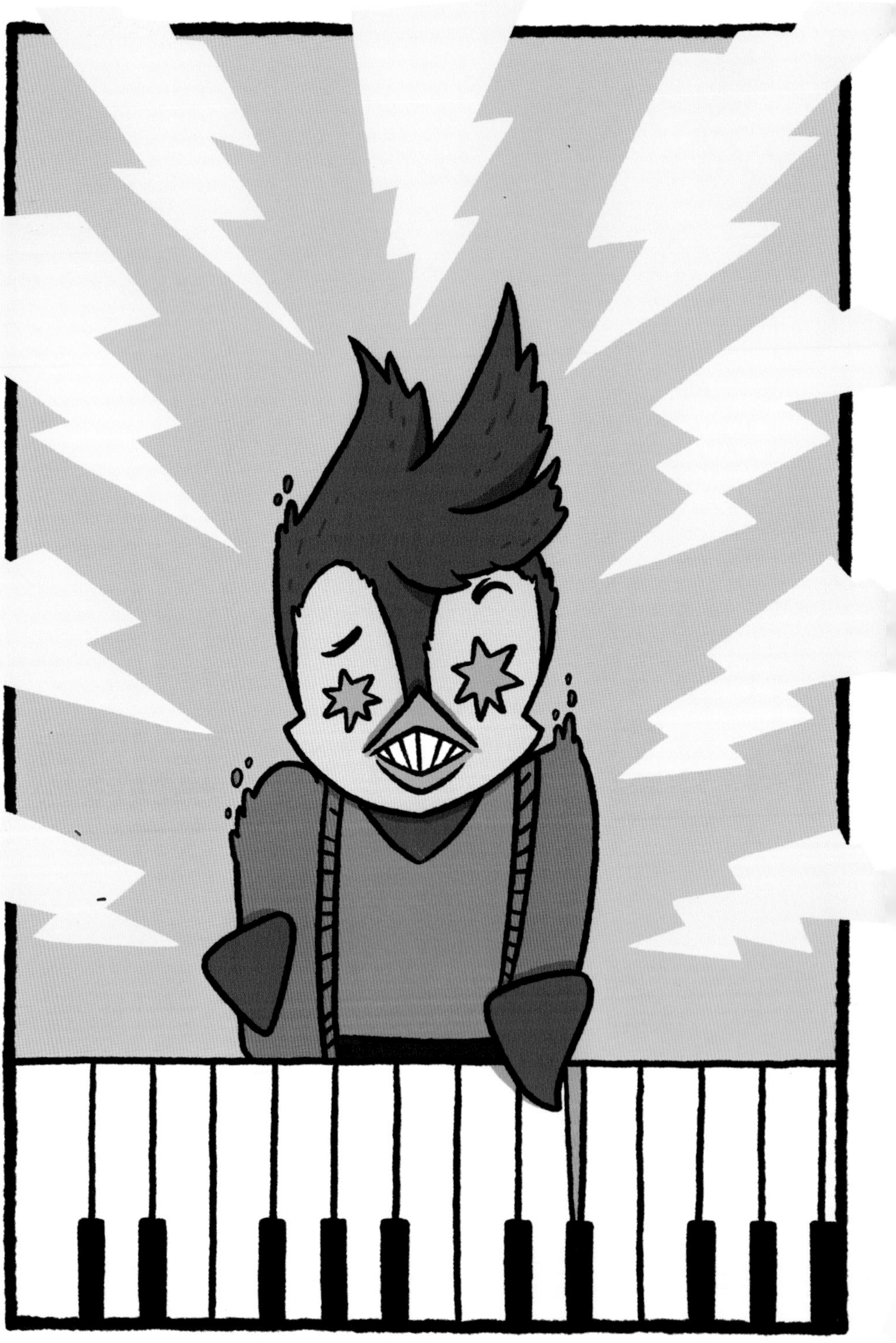

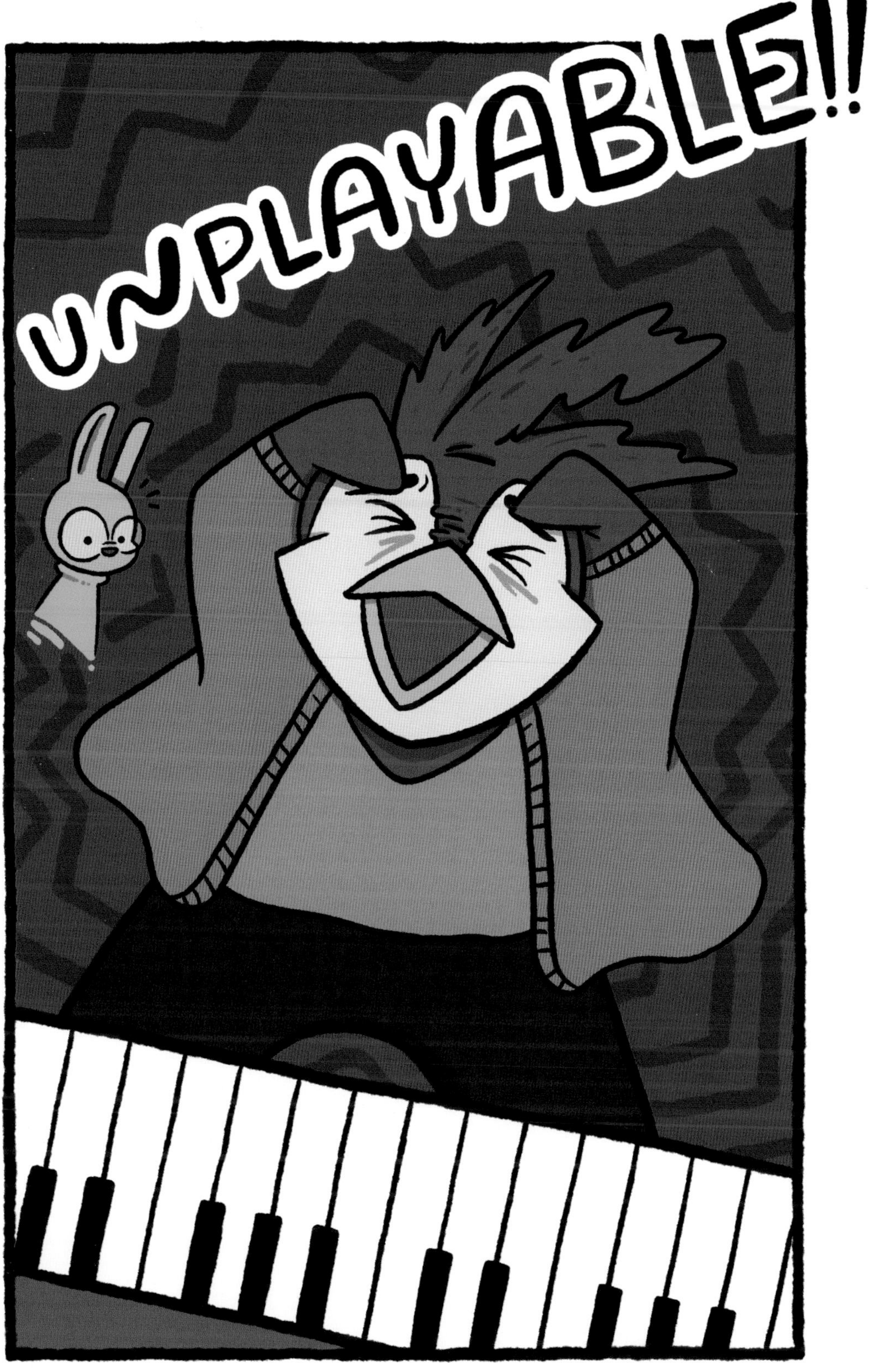
UNPLAYABLE!!

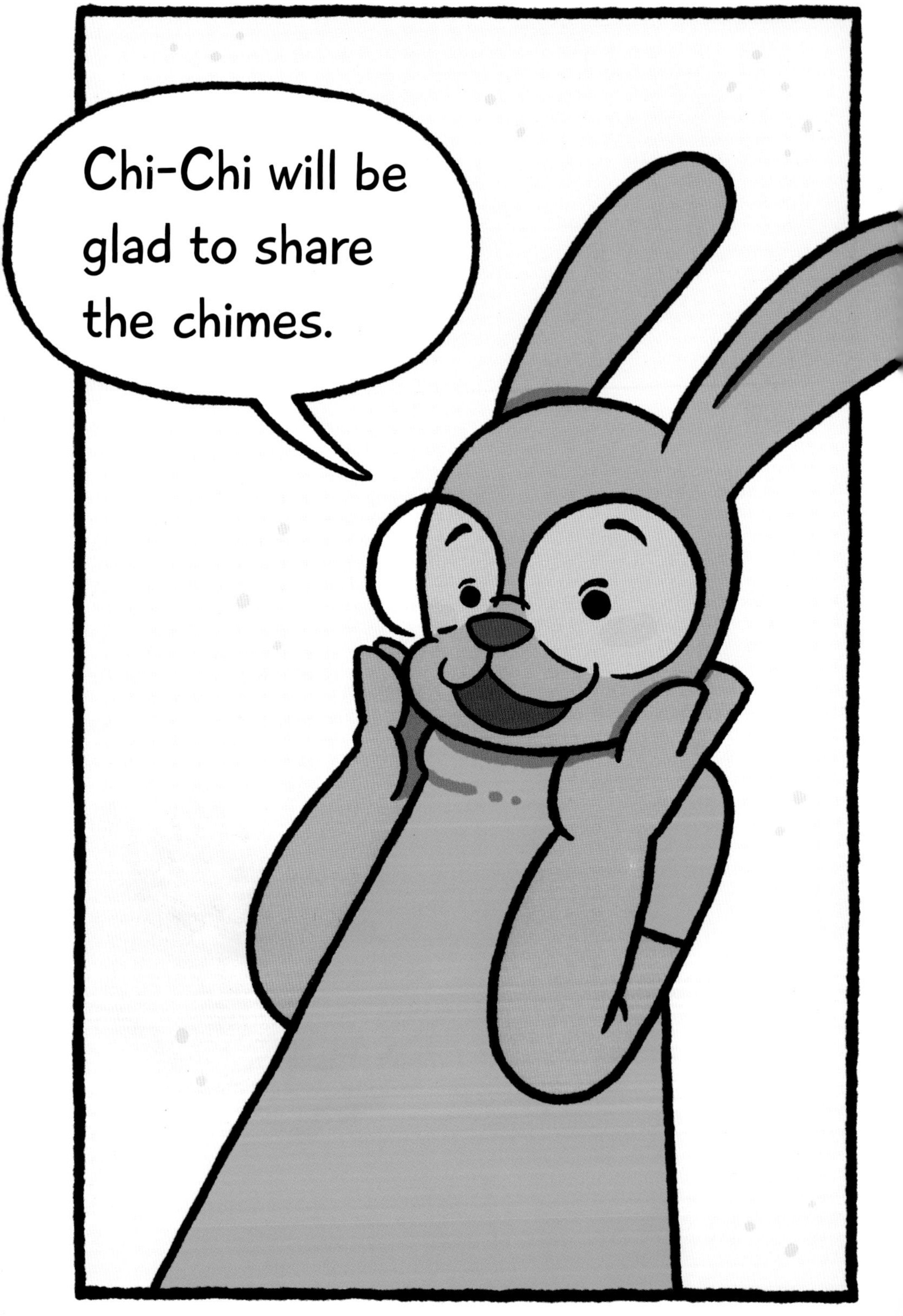
Chi-Chi will be glad to share the chimes.

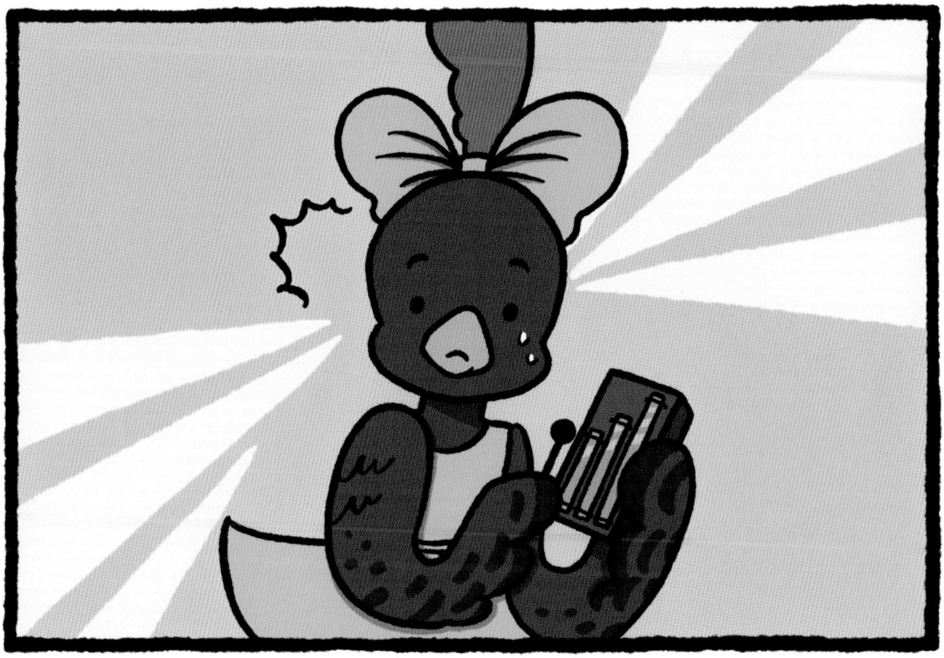

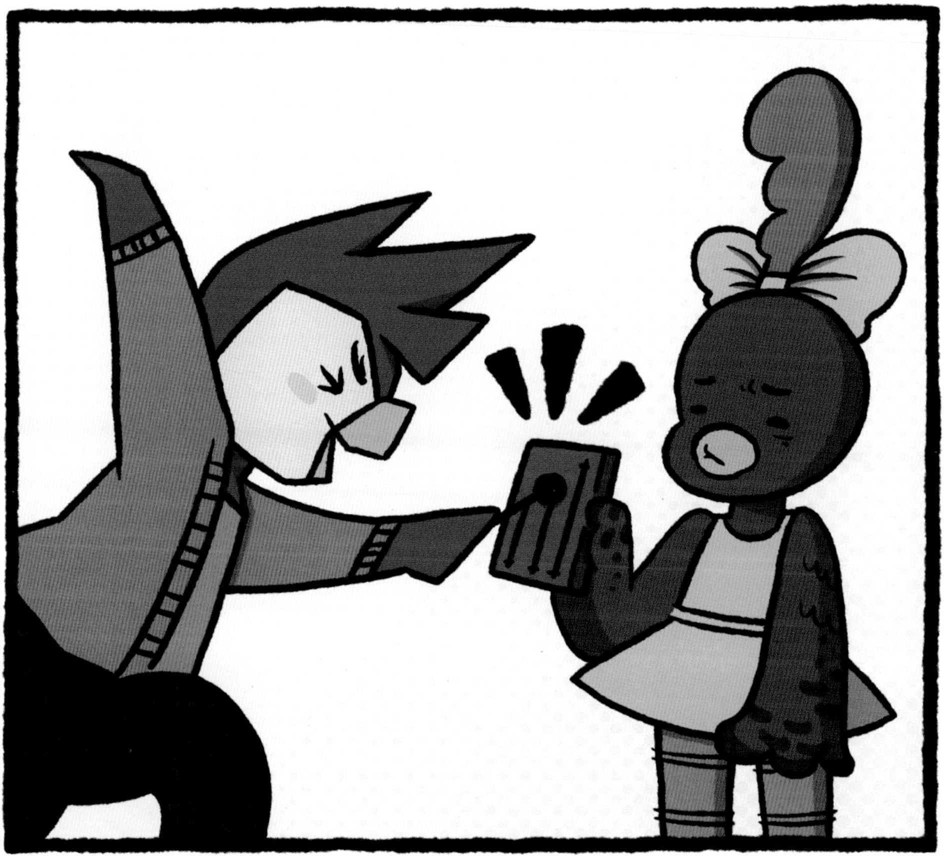

And everyone is happy. Until...

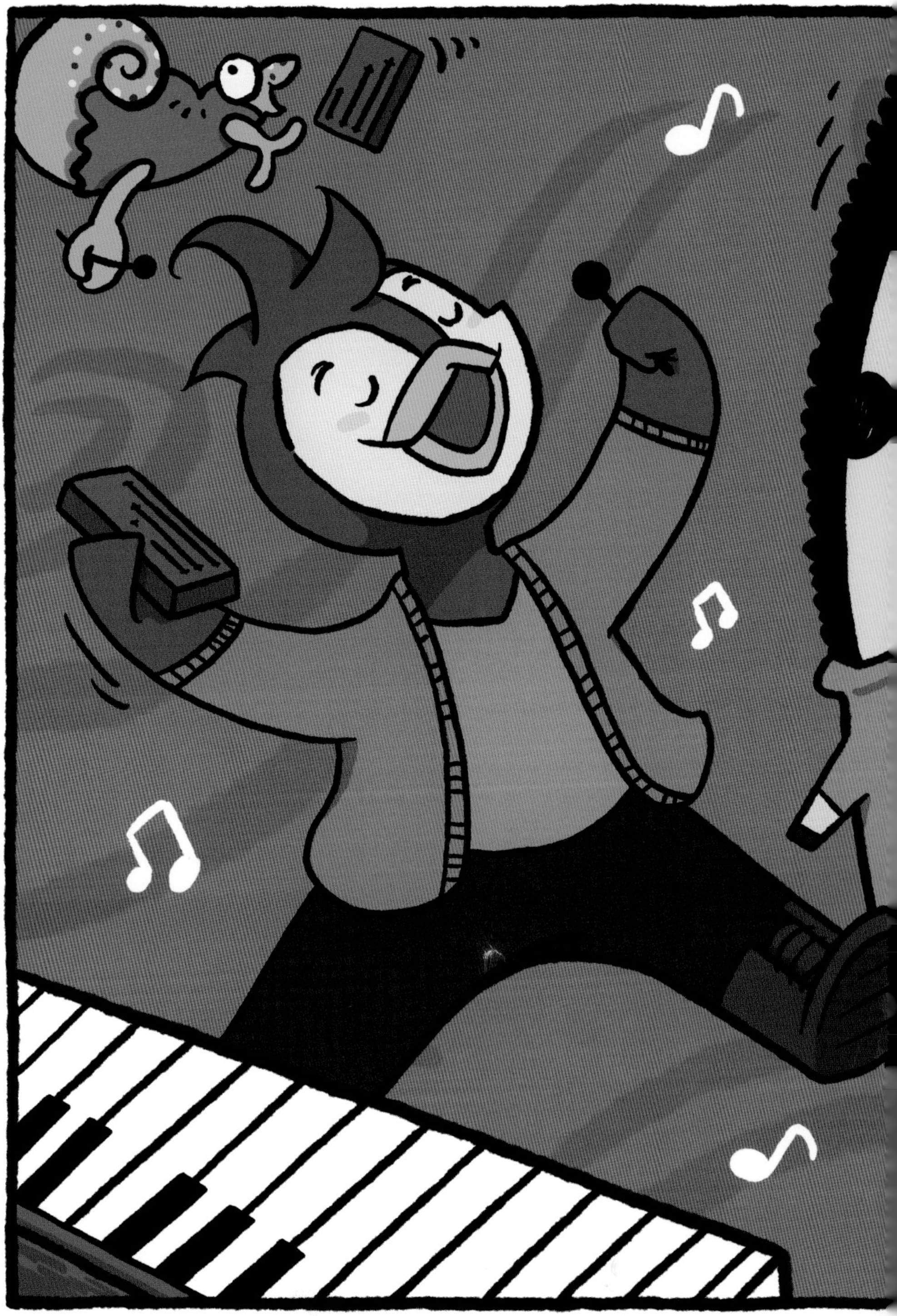

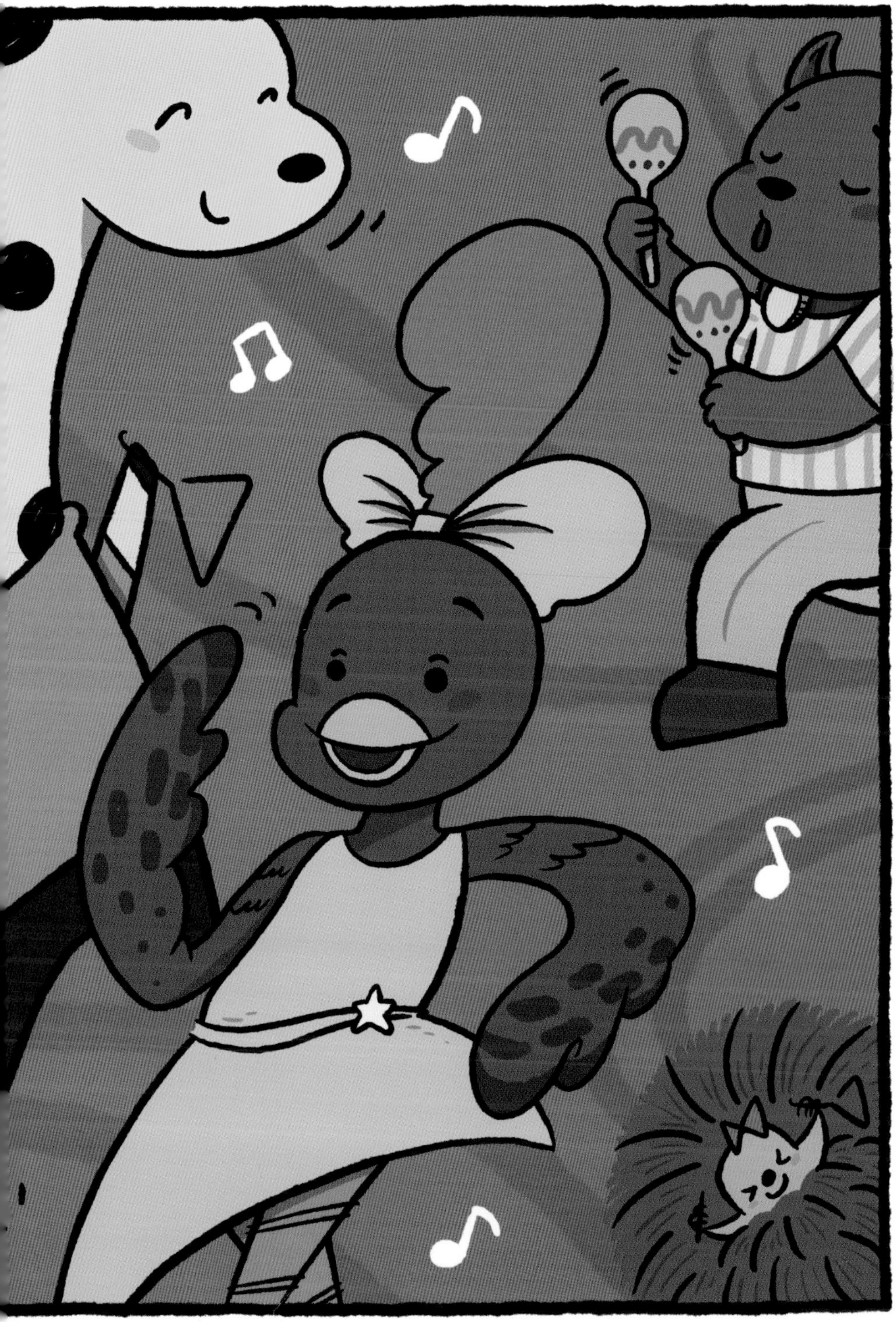

...there are cupcakes for snack.

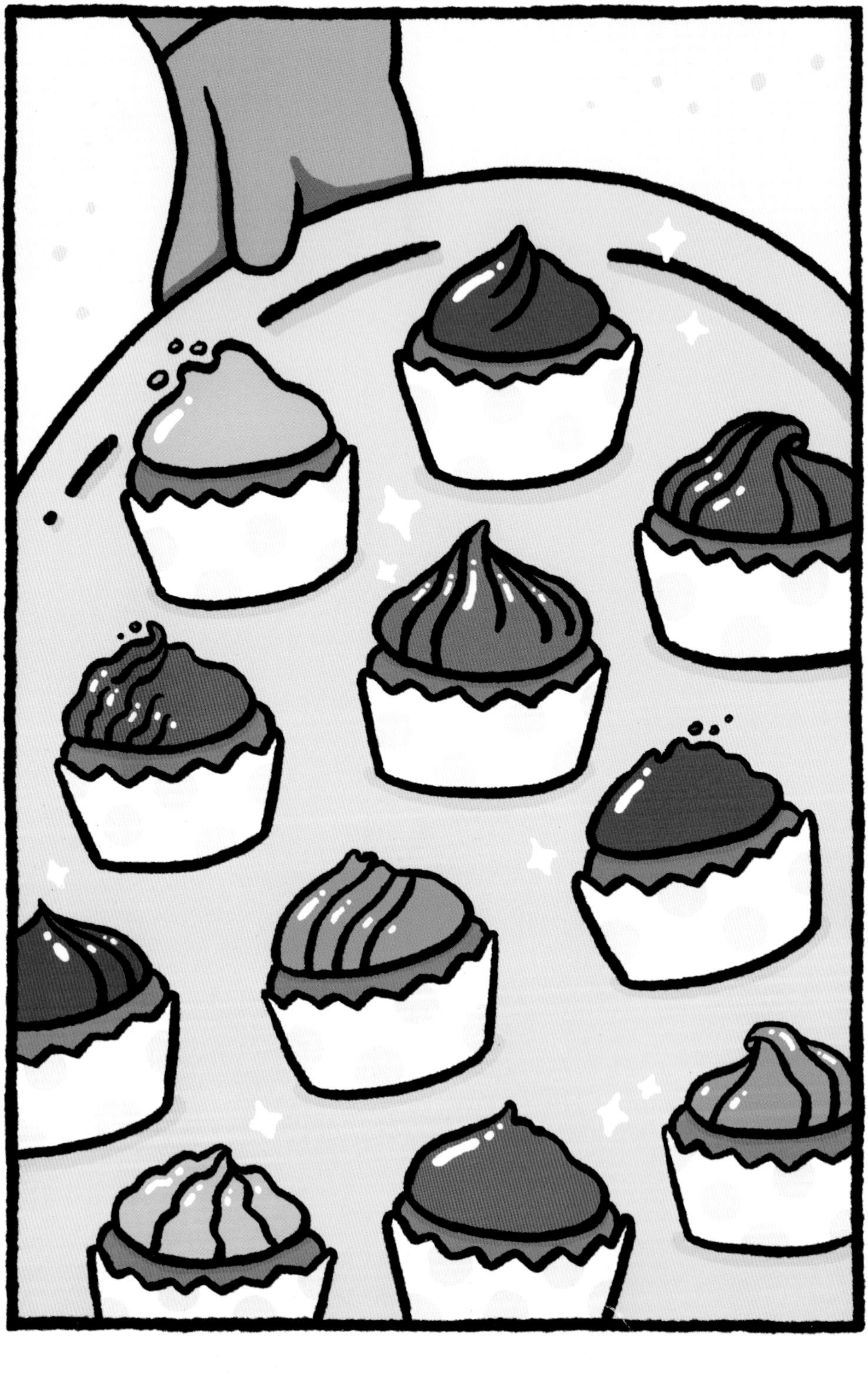

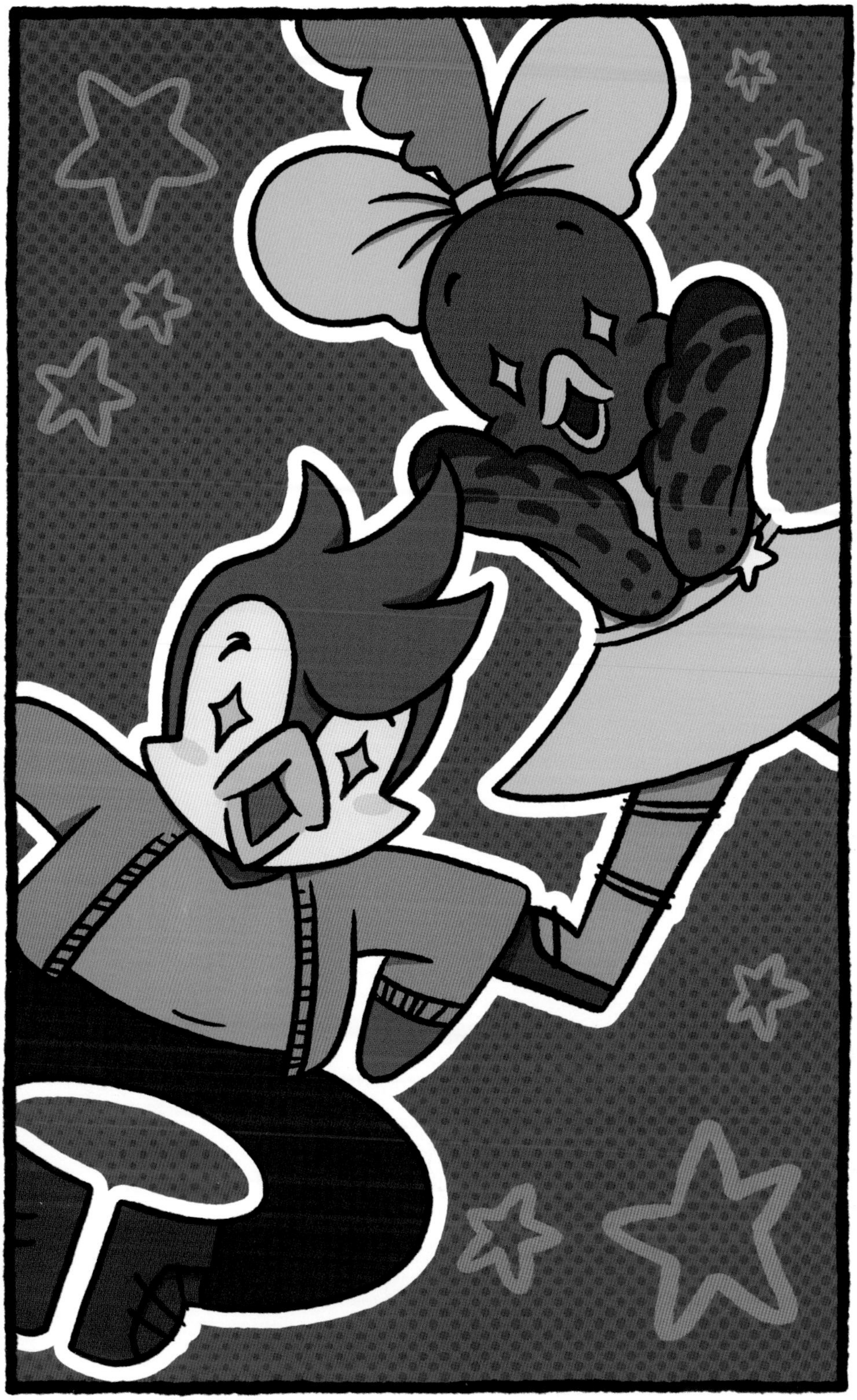

This may seem like a good thing.

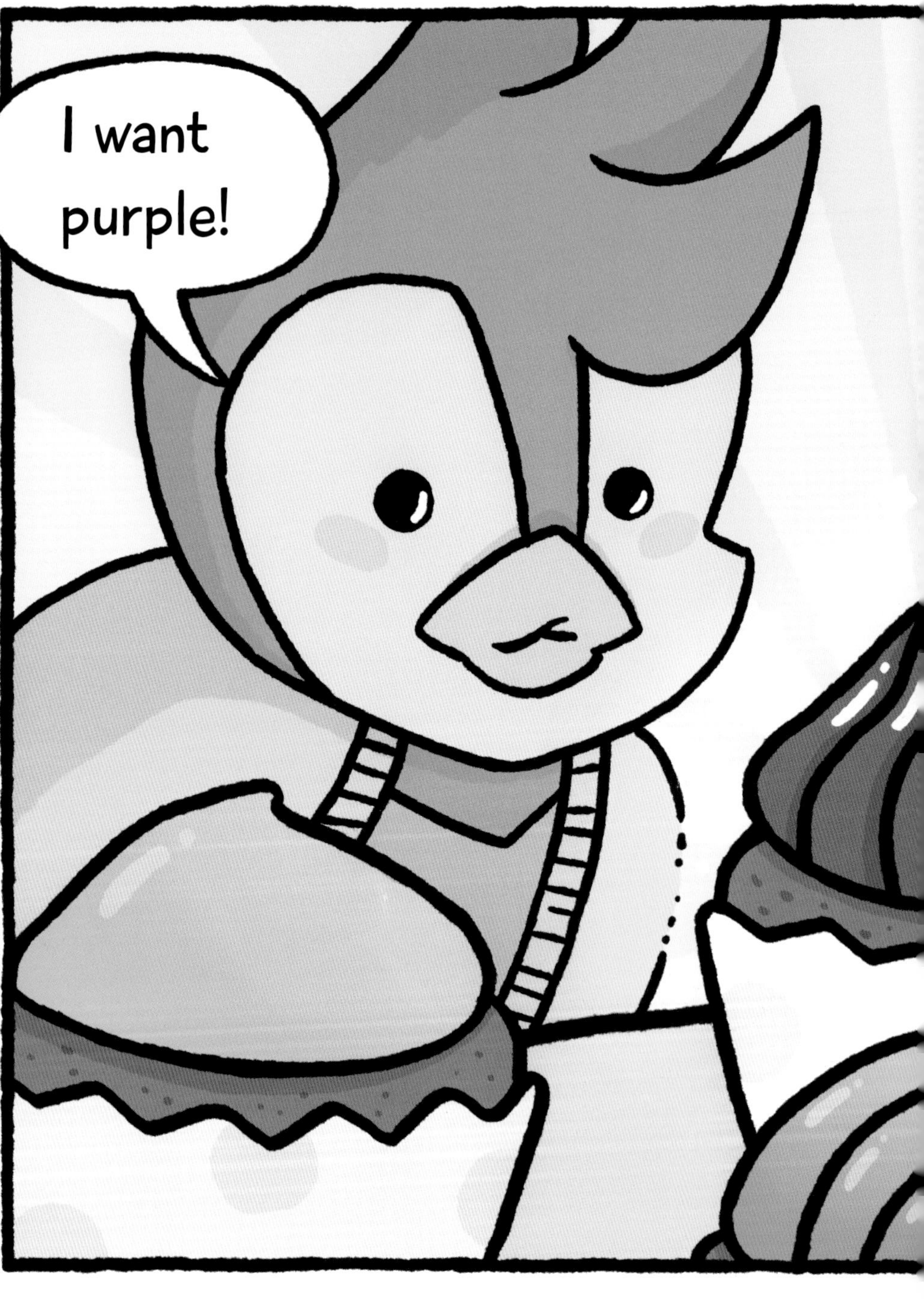
I want purple!

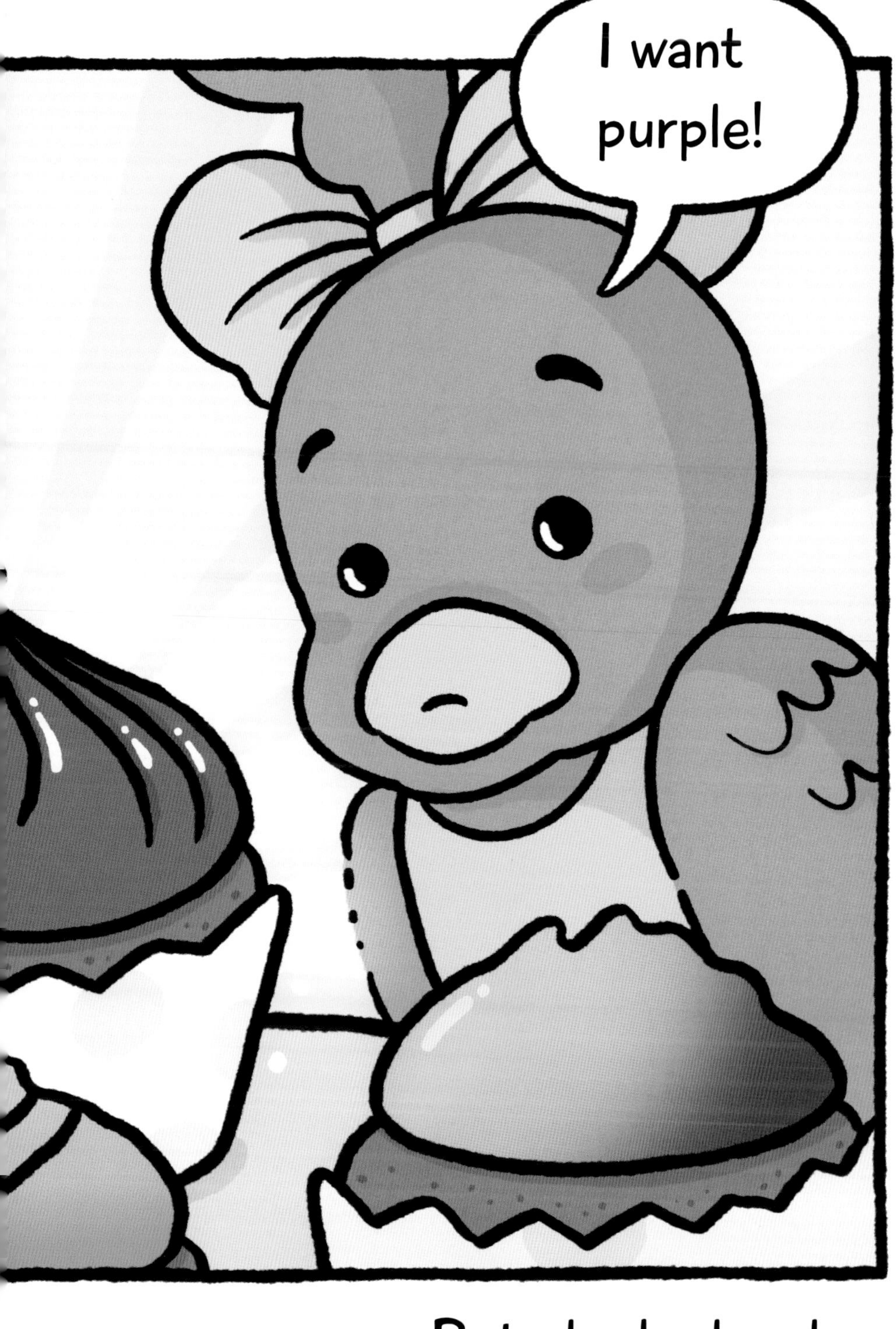
I want purple!

But…look closely.

There is only **ONE** purple cupcake.

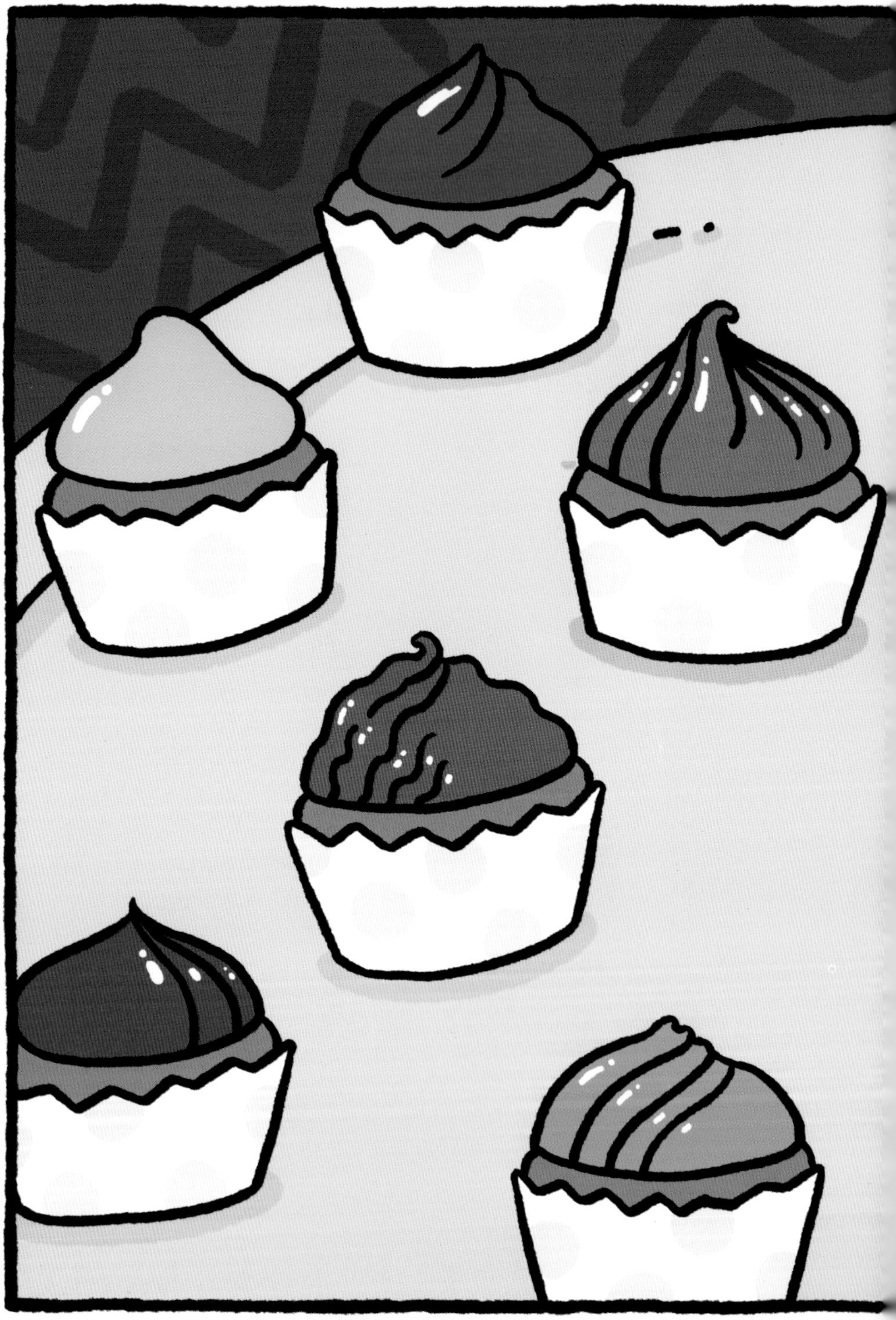

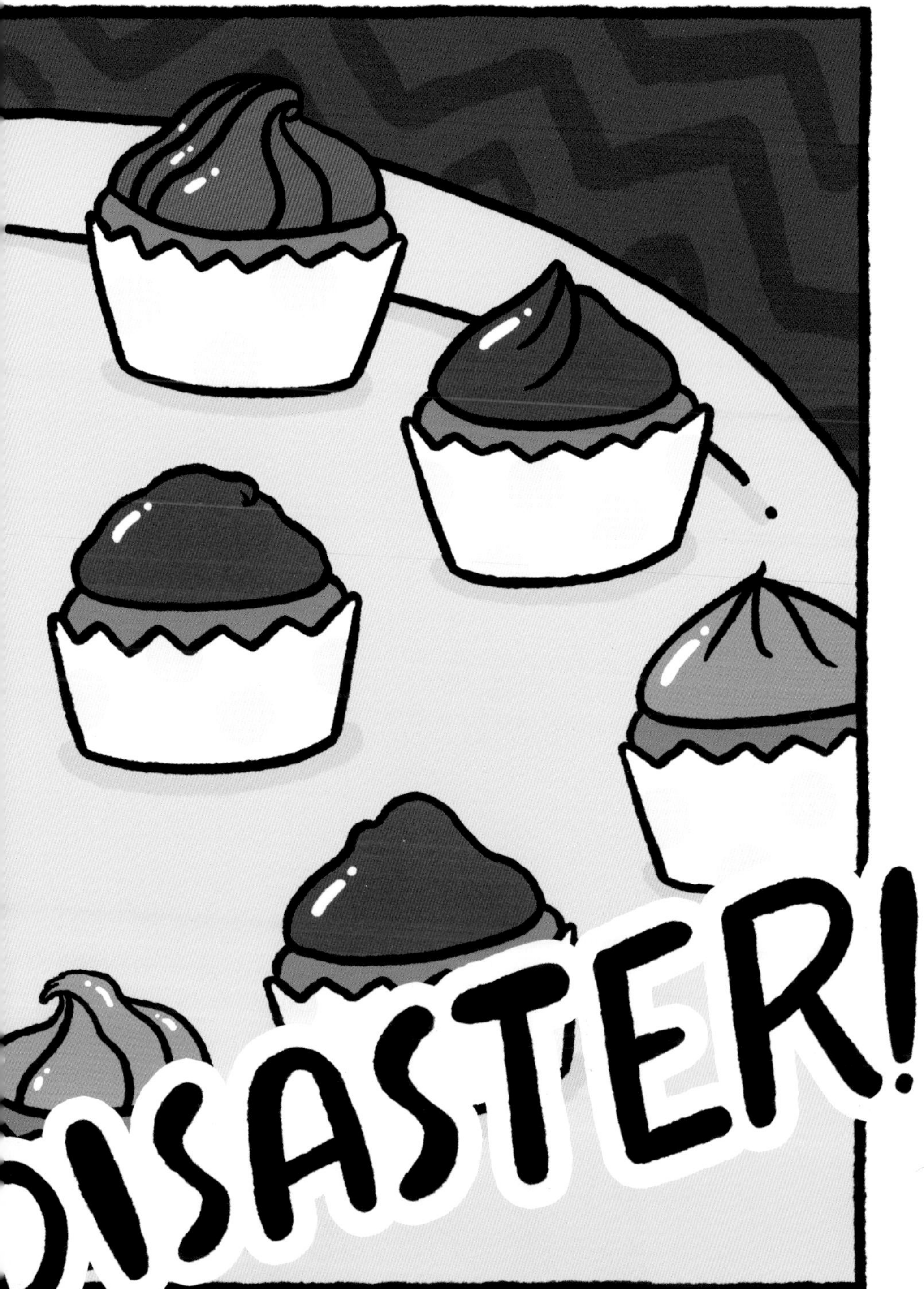
DISASTER!

This might be a problem.

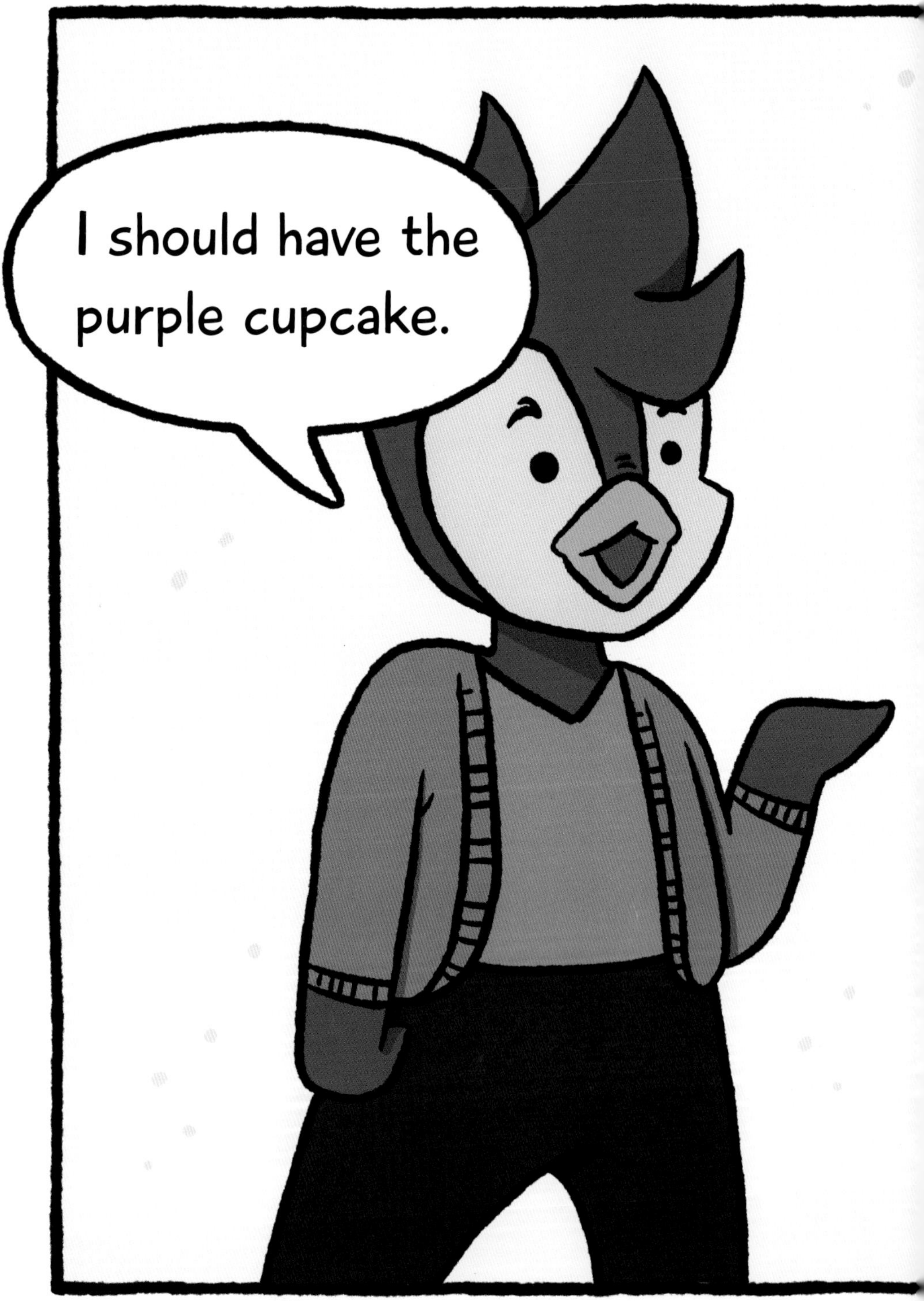
I should have the purple cupcake.

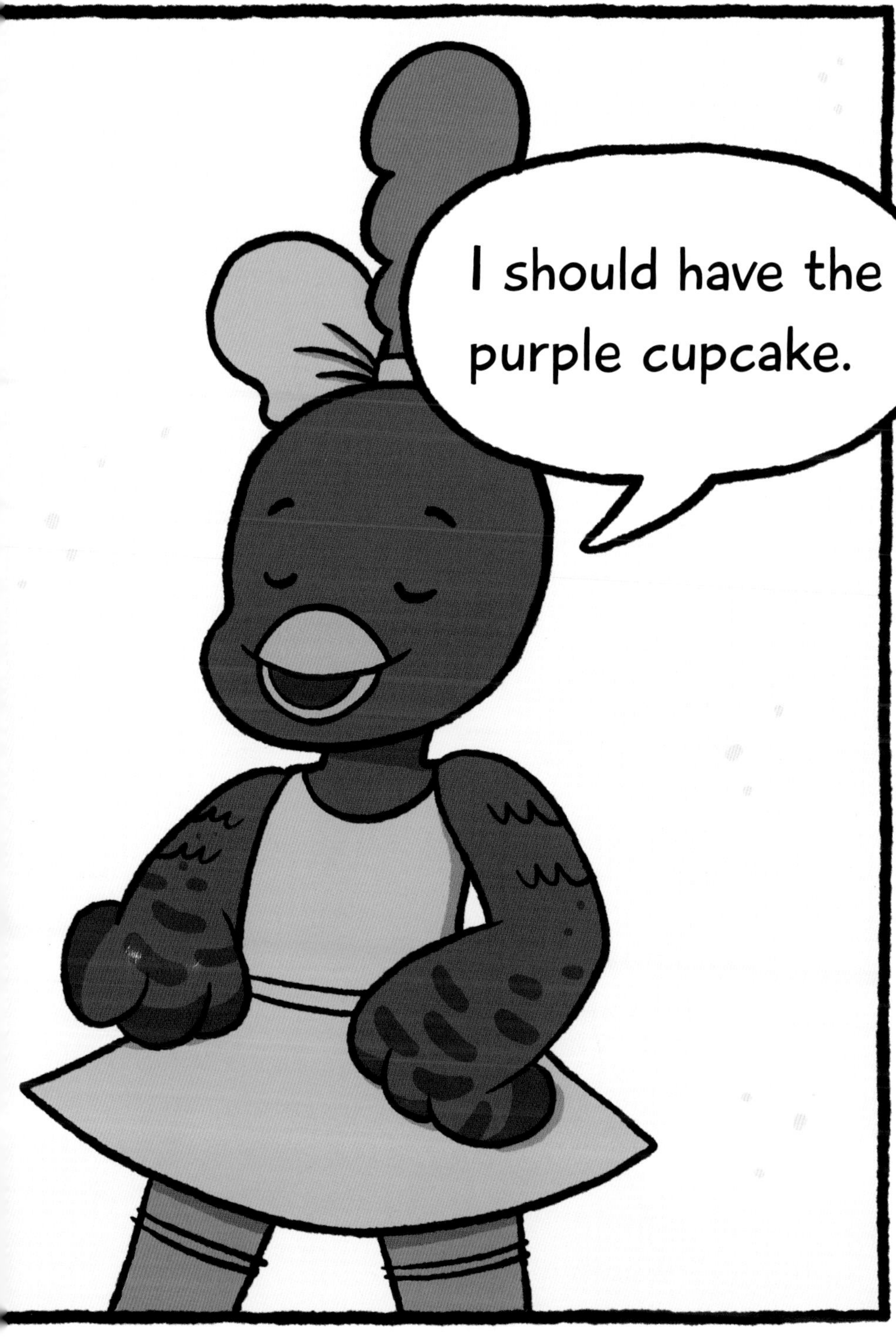
I should have the purple cupcake.

Pey-Pey explains.

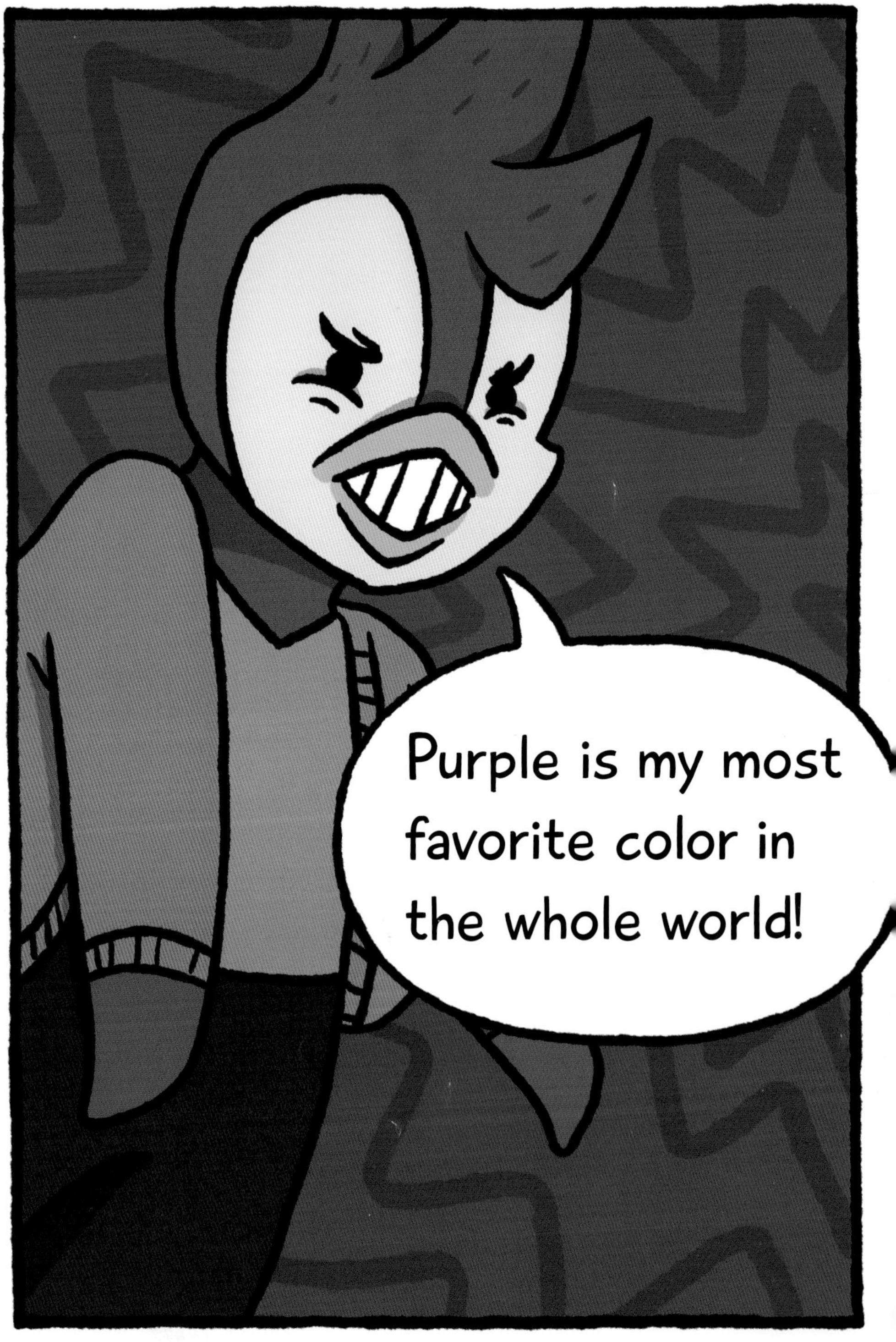
Purple is my most favorite color in the whole world!

Chi-Chi explains.

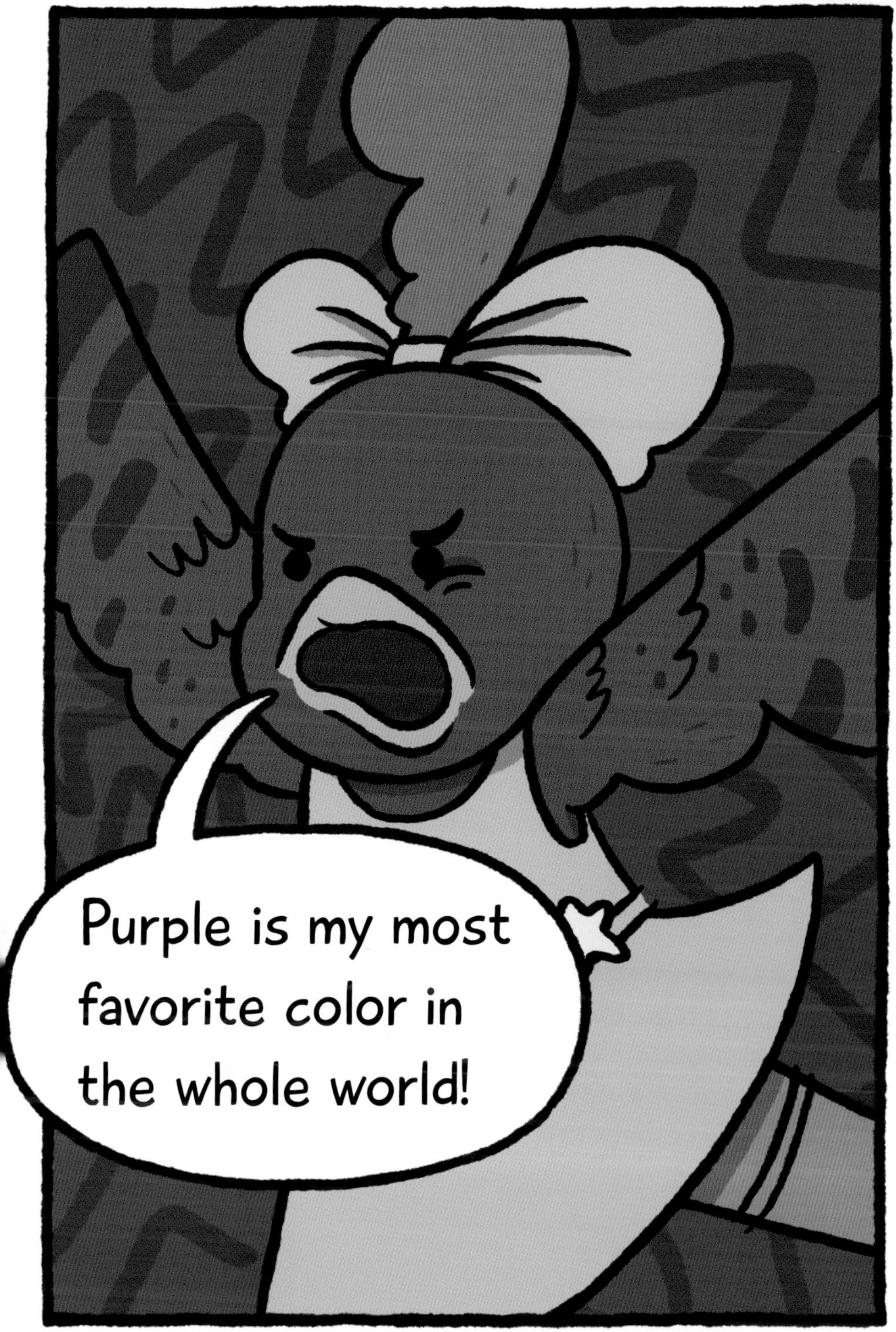
Purple is my most favorite color in the whole world!

Pey-Pey peeps.

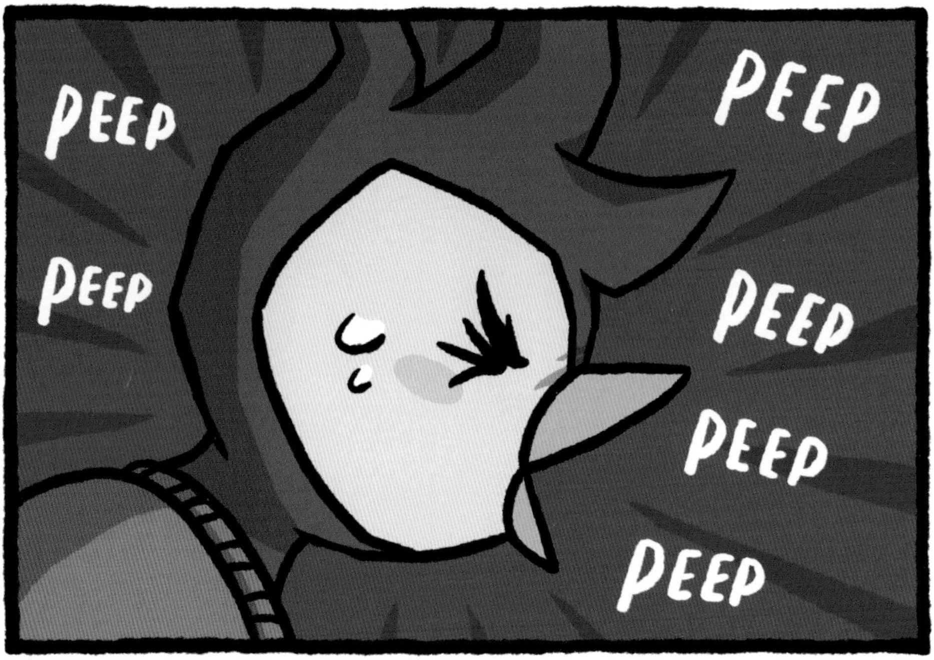
PEEP
PEEP
PEEP
PEEP
PEEP
PEEP

Chi-Chi chirps.

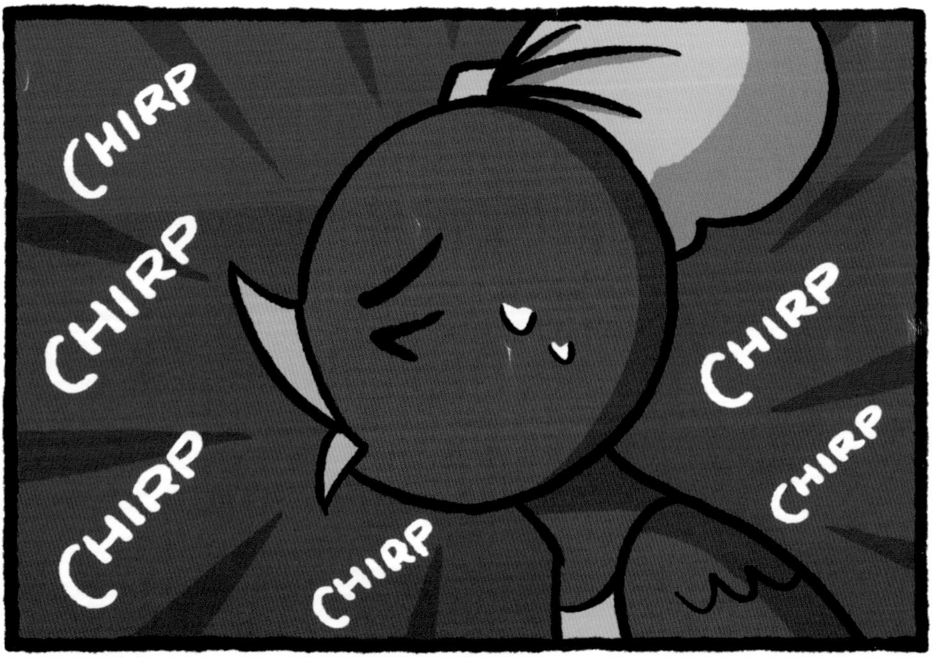
CHIRP
CHIRP
CHIRP
CHIRP
CHIRP
CHIRP

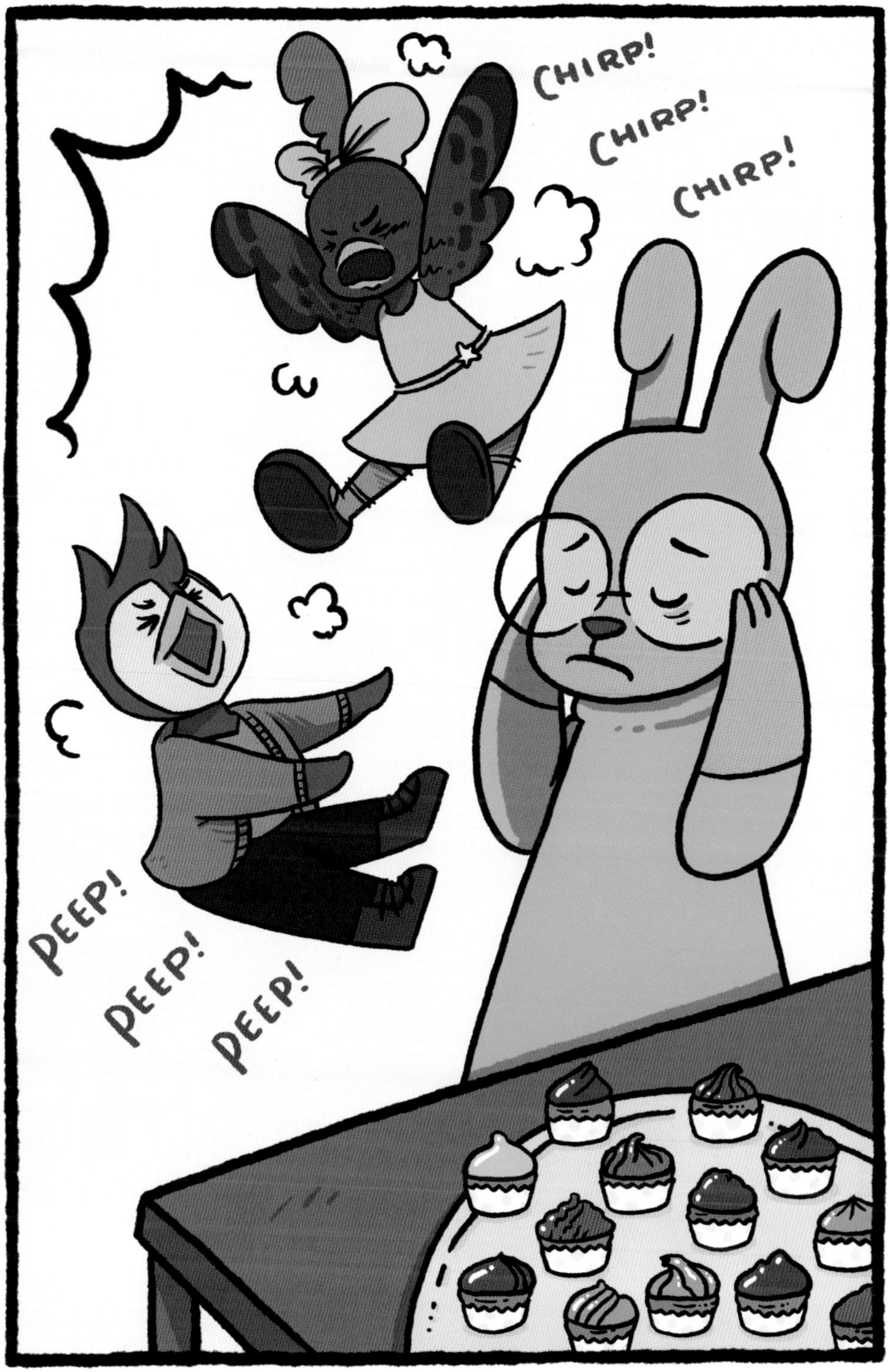
CHIRP!
CHIRP!
CHIRP!
PEEP!
PEEP!
PEEP!

No solution is in sight.

But then Chi-Chi has a great idea.

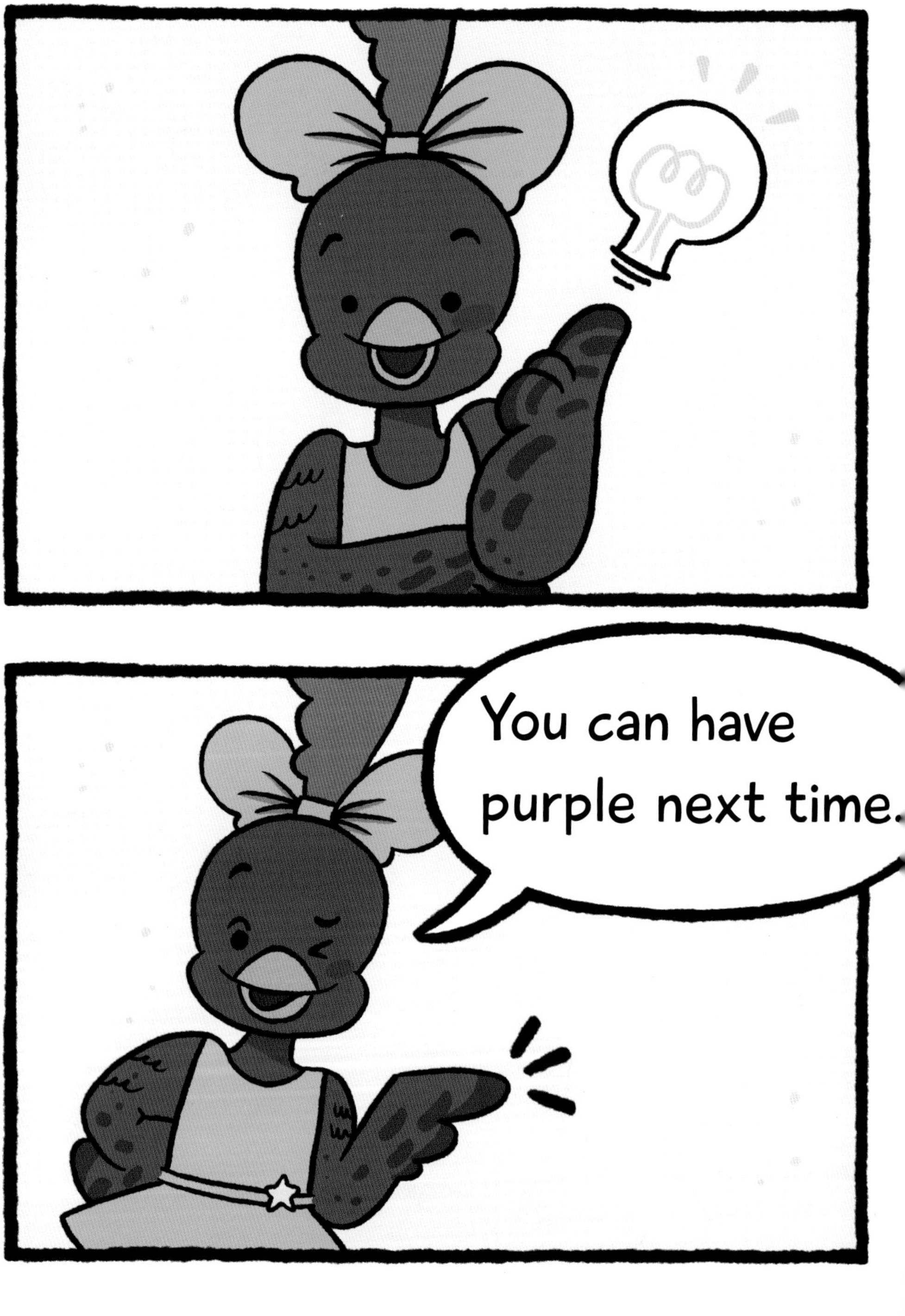
You can have purple next time.

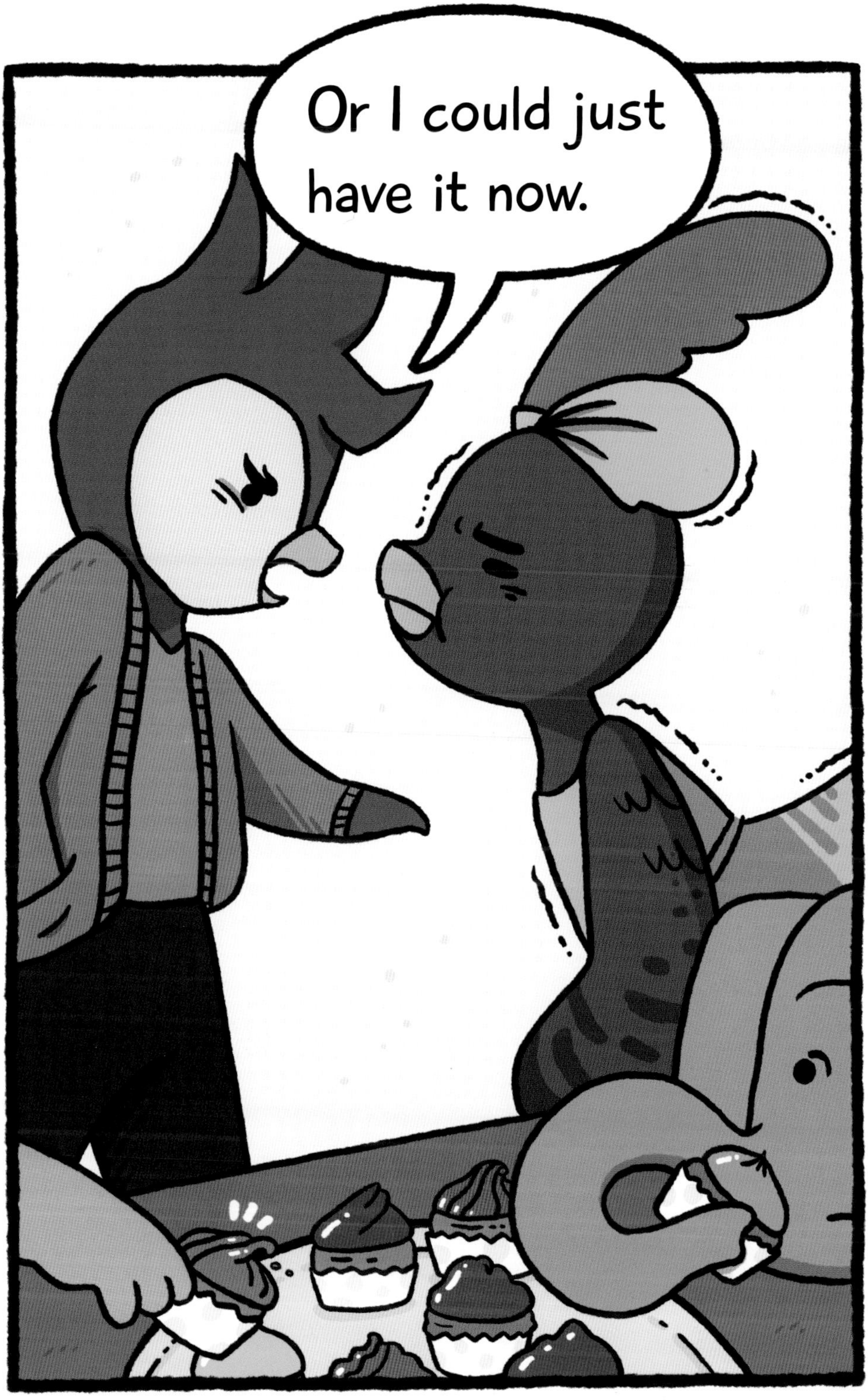
Or I could just have it now.

That solution will not work.

Chi-Chi and Pey-Pey think hard.

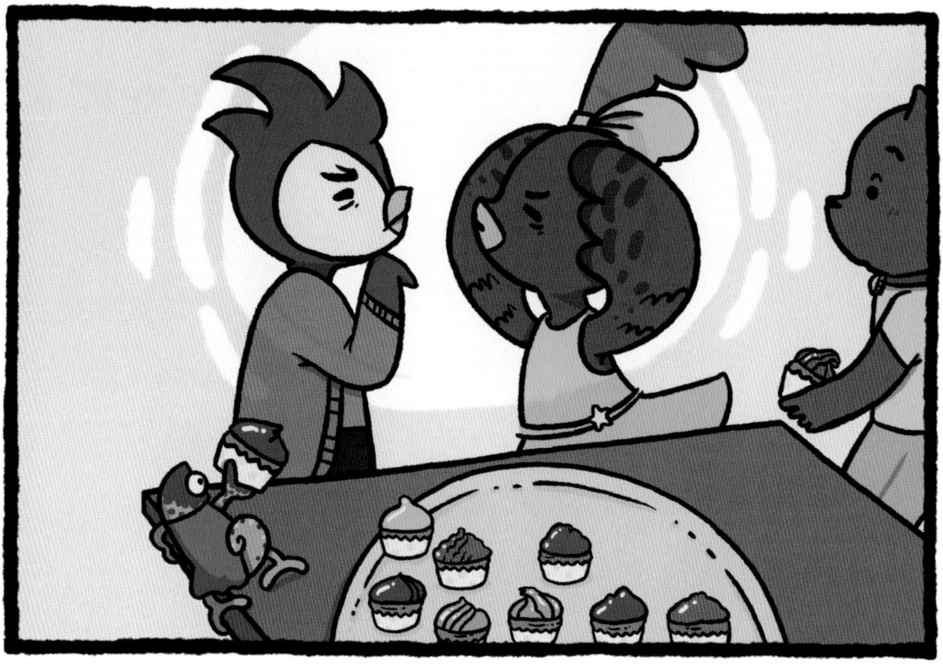

They work to figure out a solution.

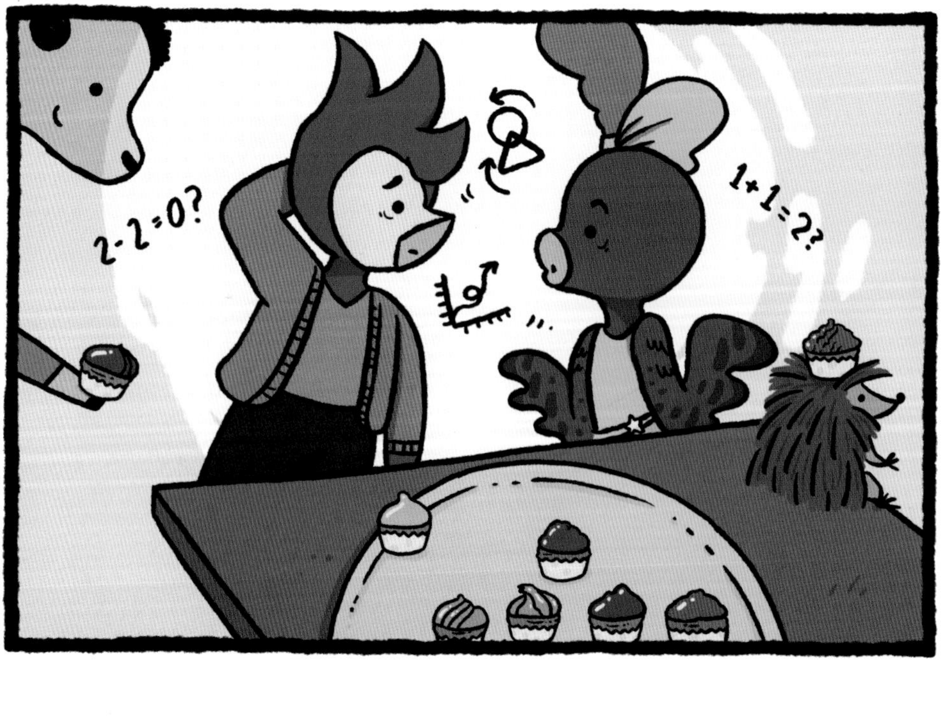
2-2=0?
1+1=2??

After many ideas,

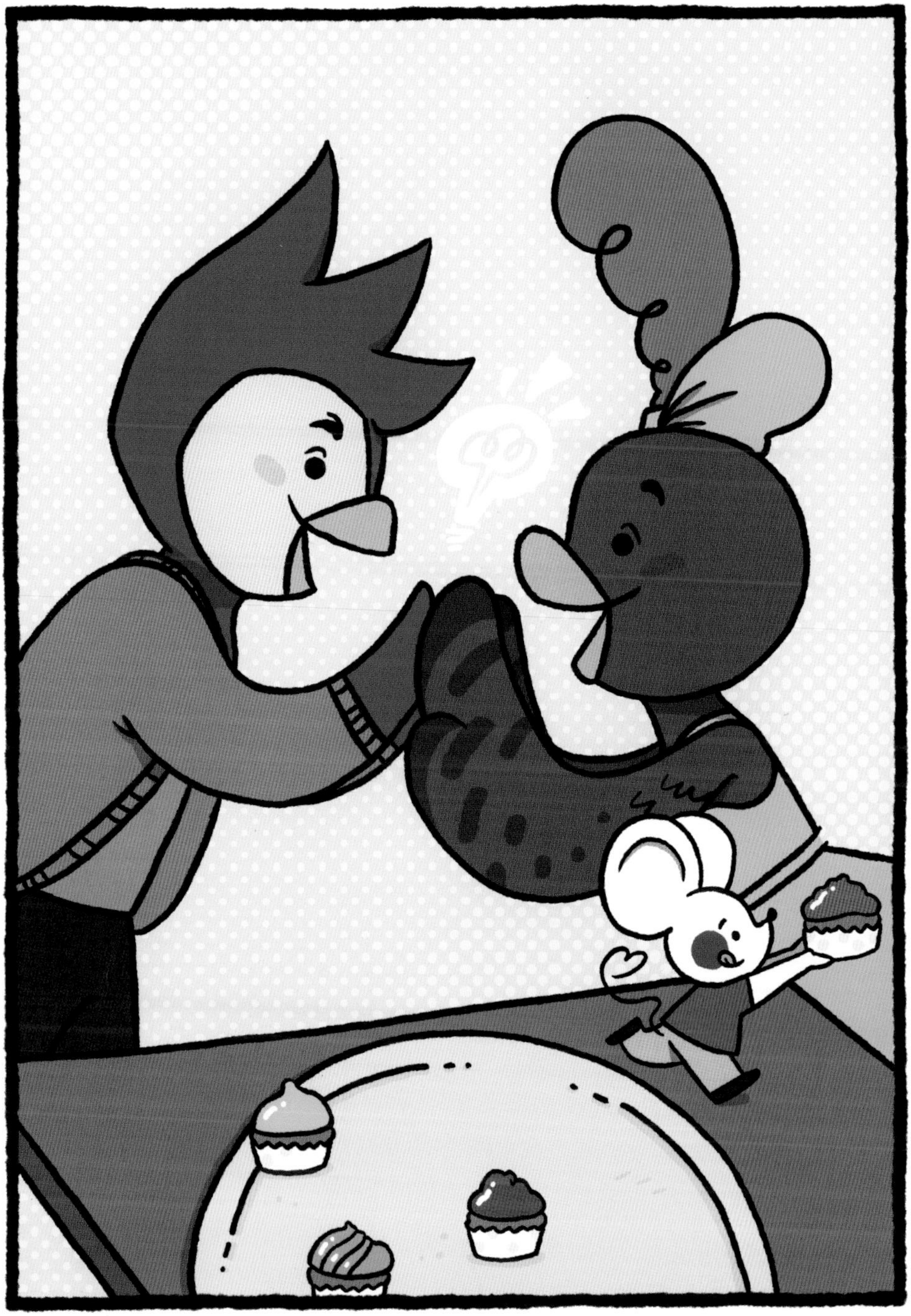

they finally agree.

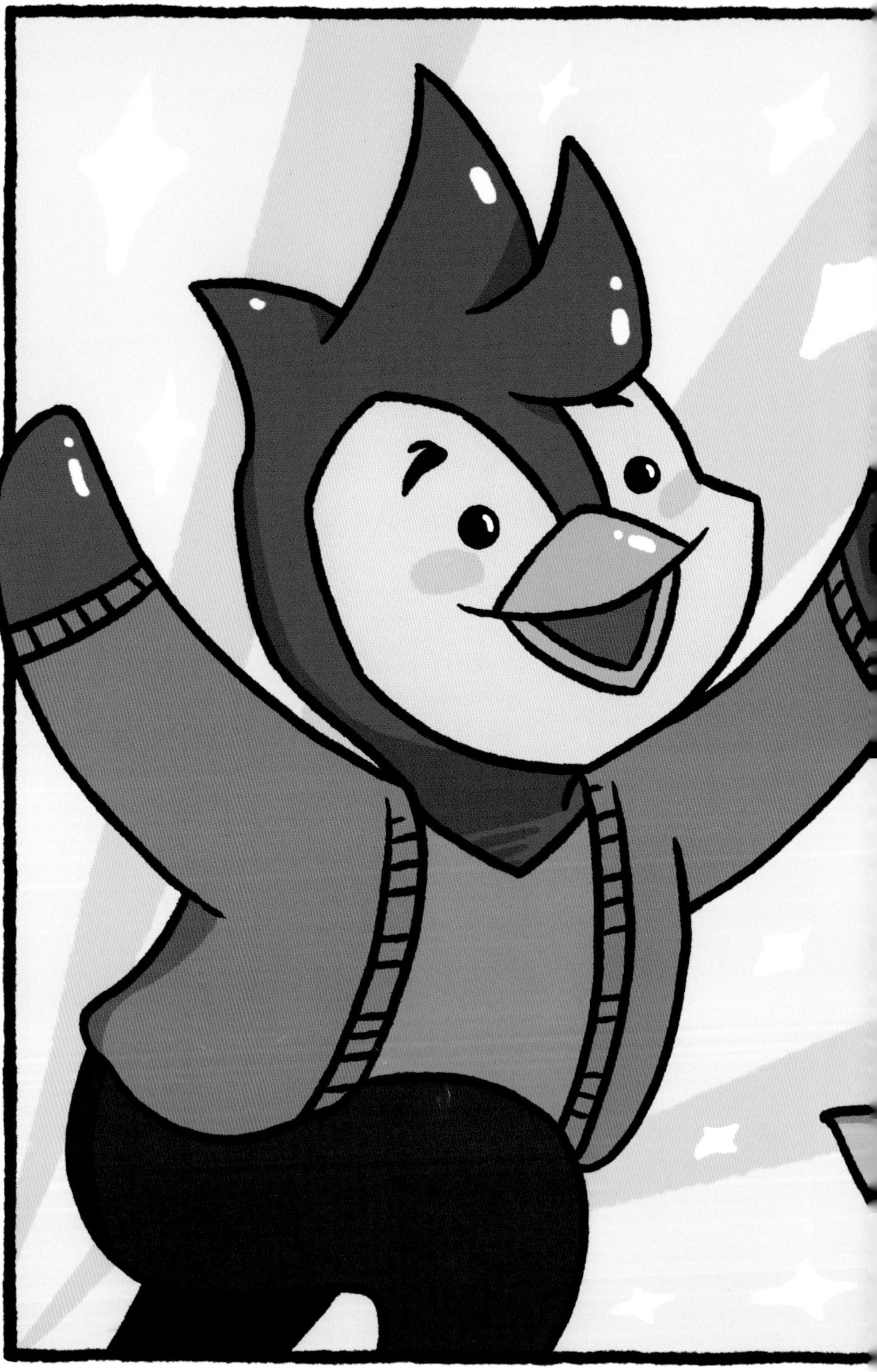

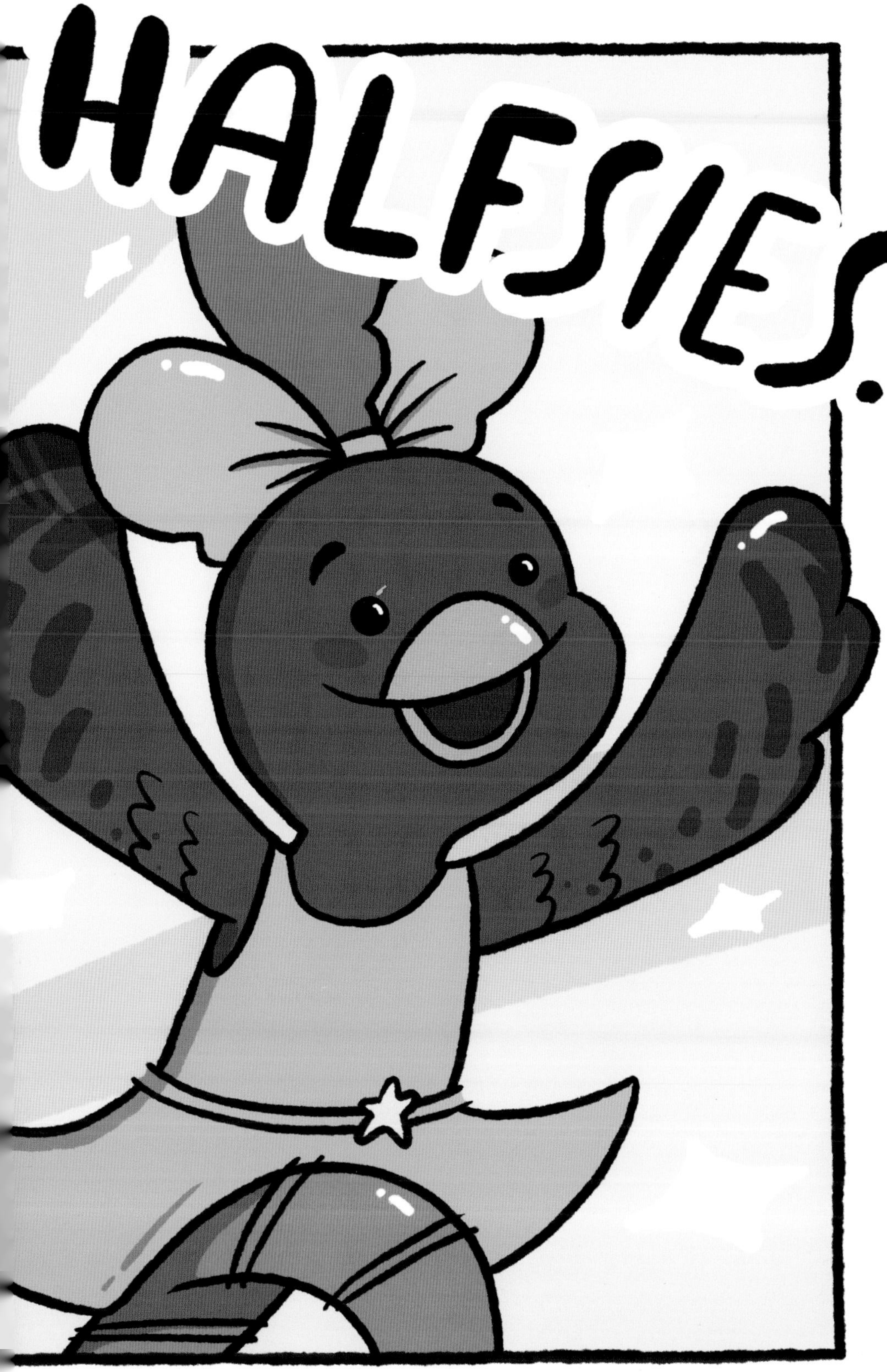
HALFSIES.

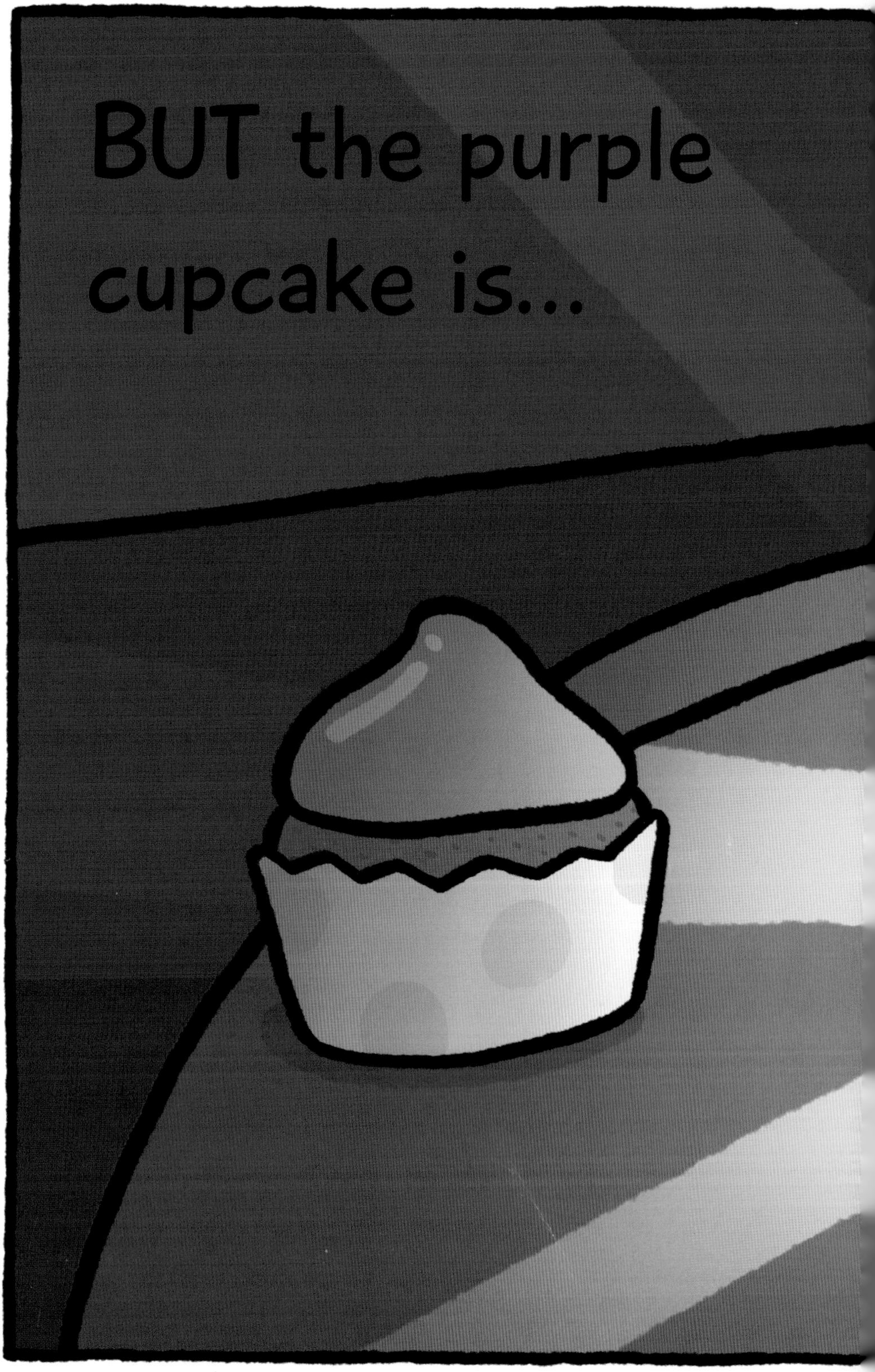
BUT the purple cupcake is...

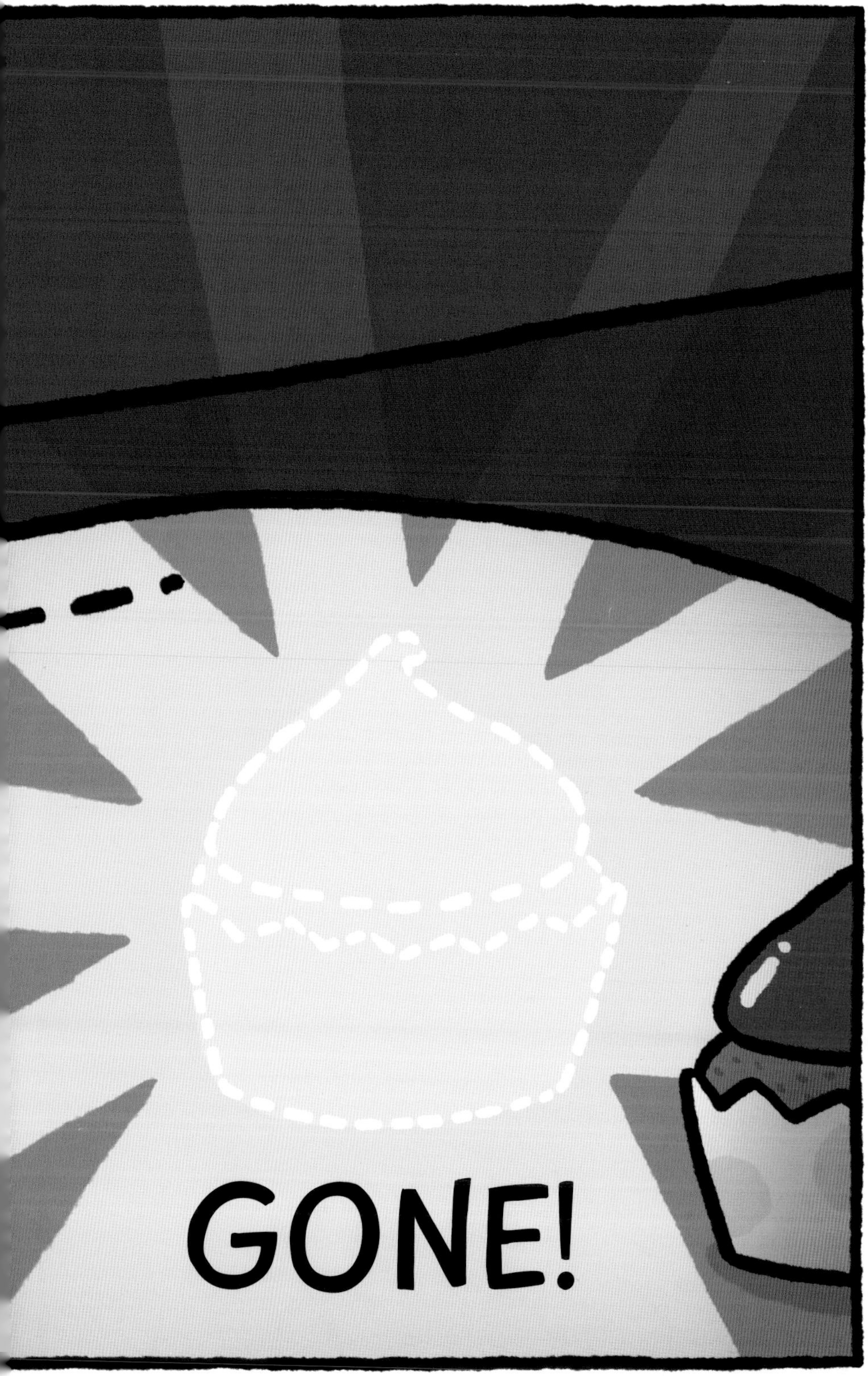
GONE!

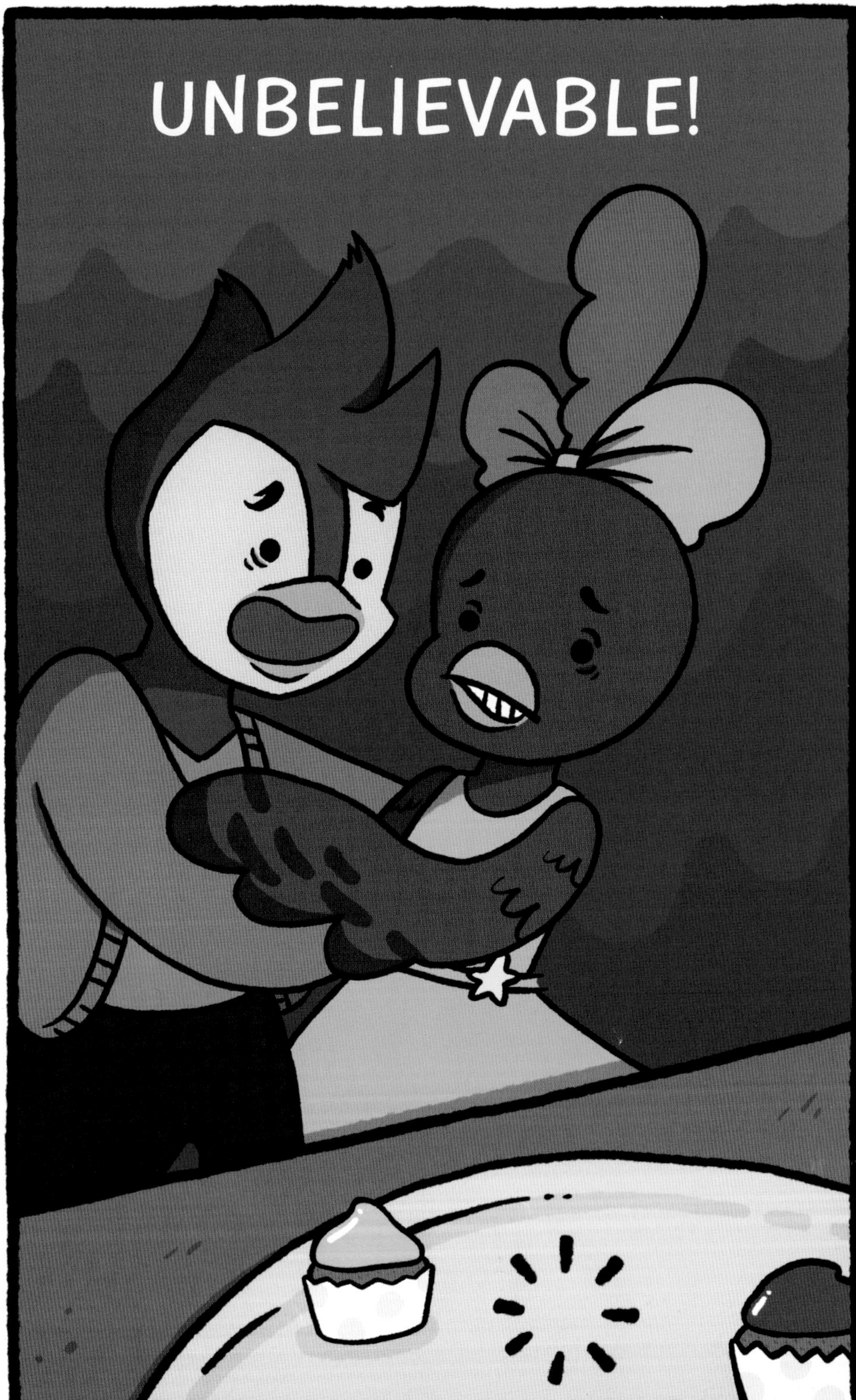
UNBELIEVABLE!

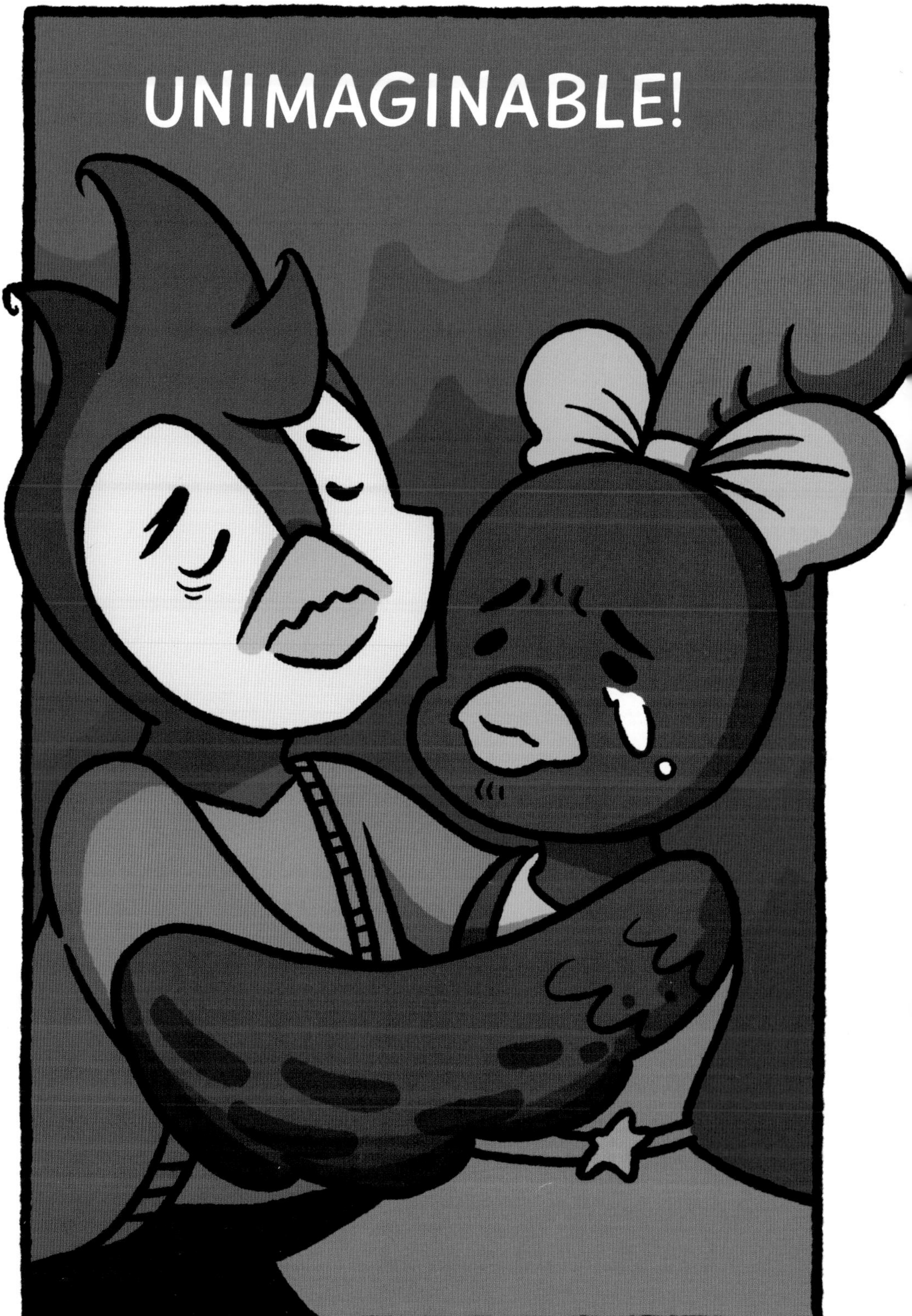
UNIMAGINABLE!

Who would eat the purple cupcake?

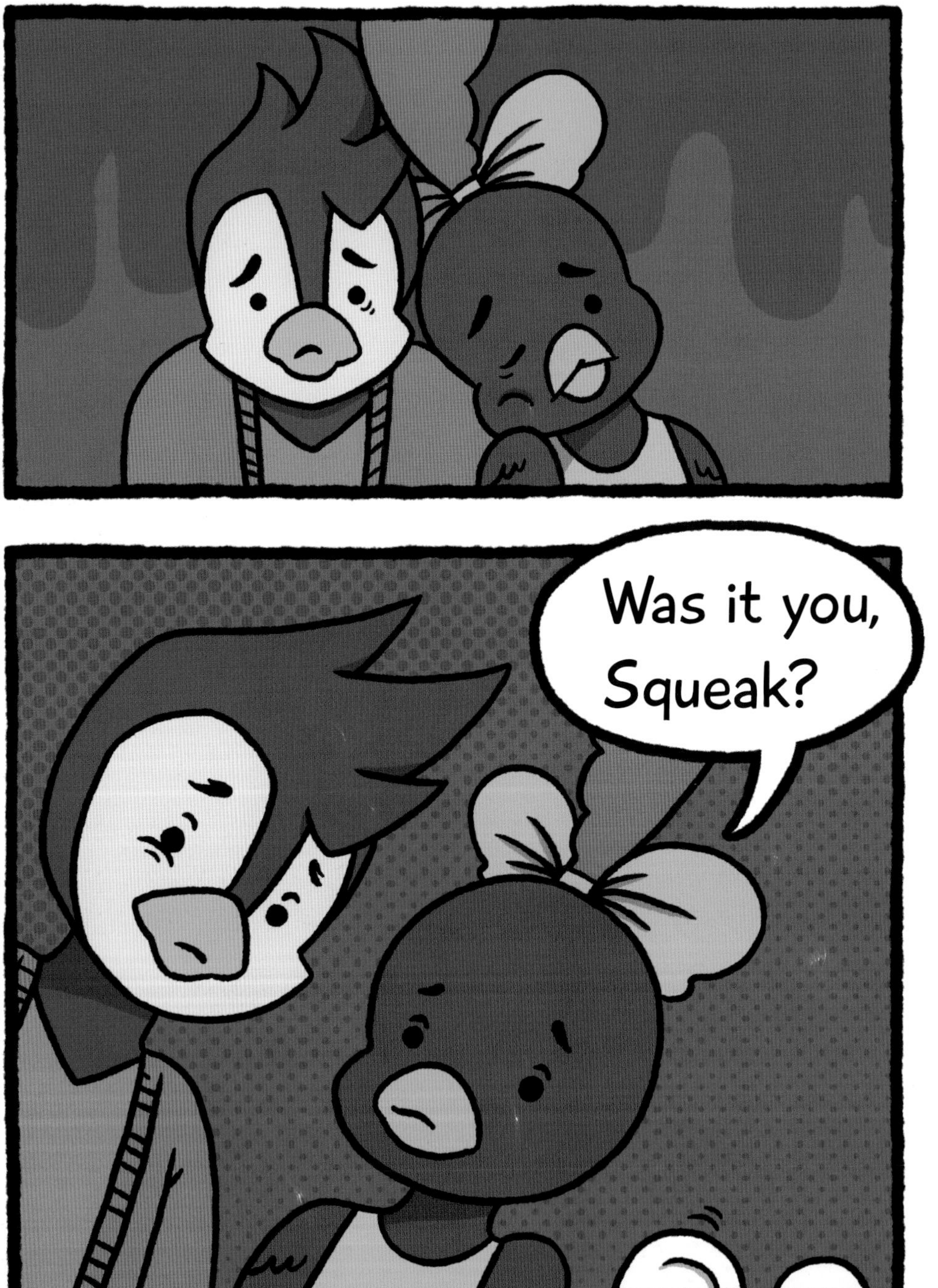
Was it you, Squeak?

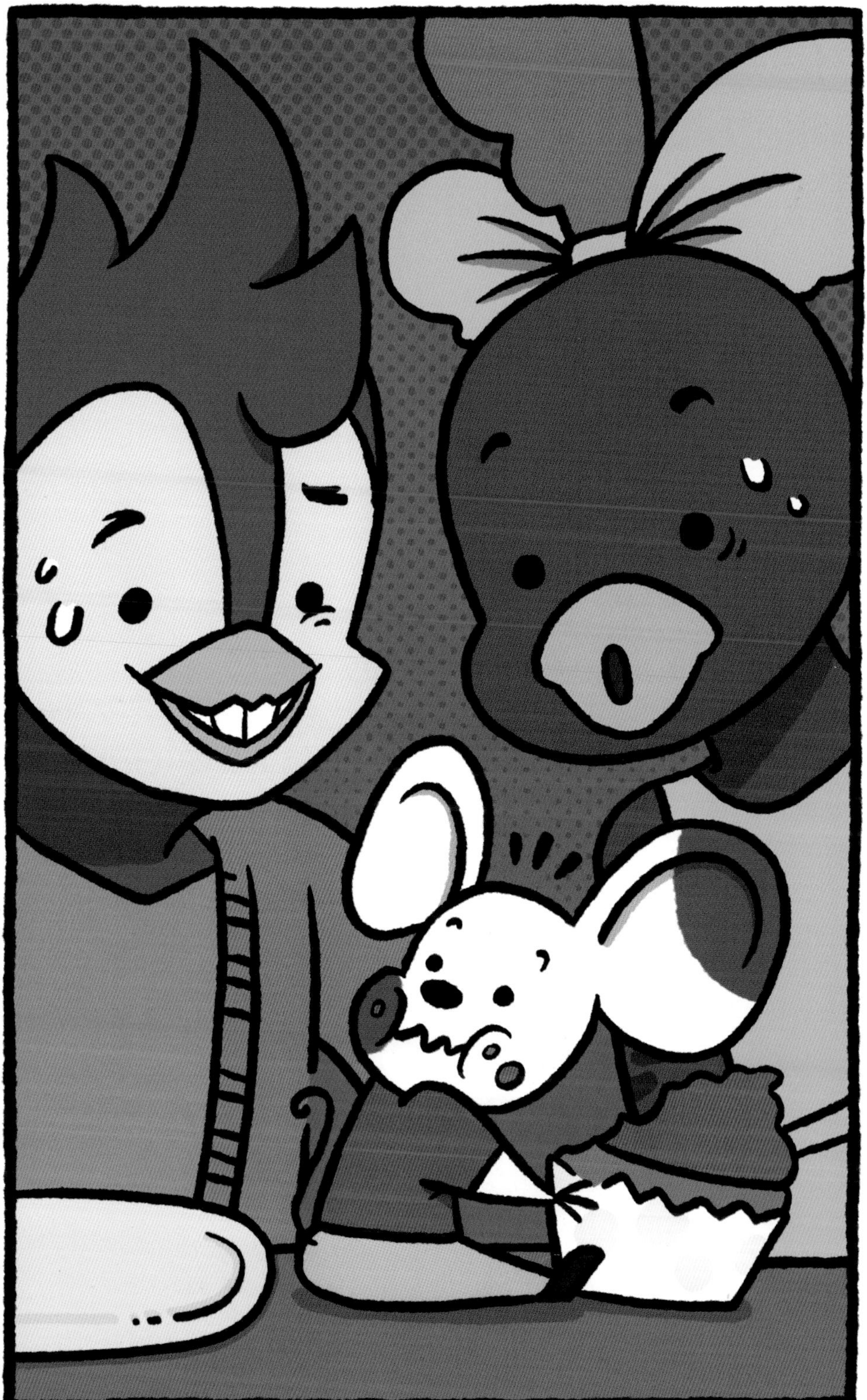

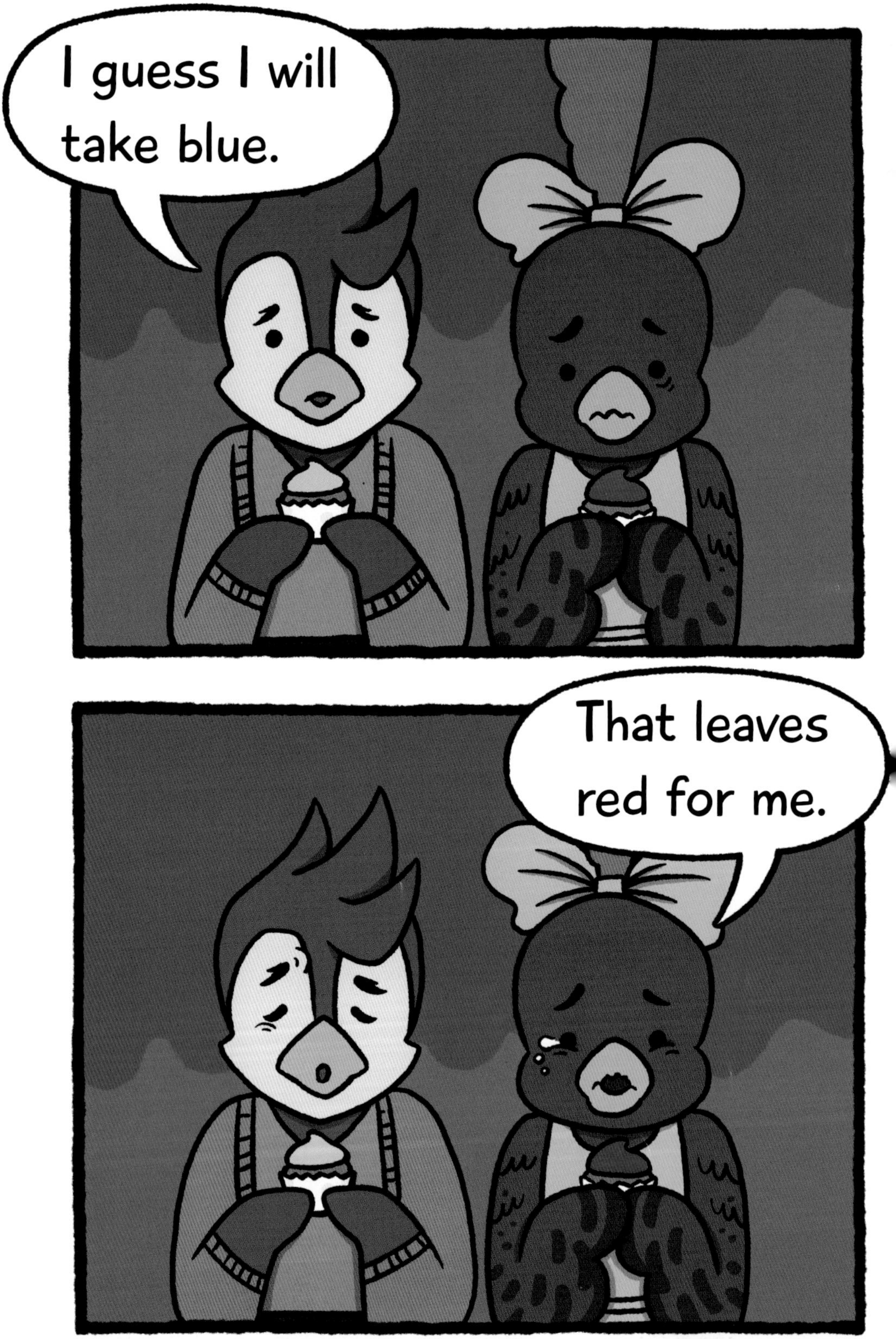
I guess I will take blue.
That leaves red for me.

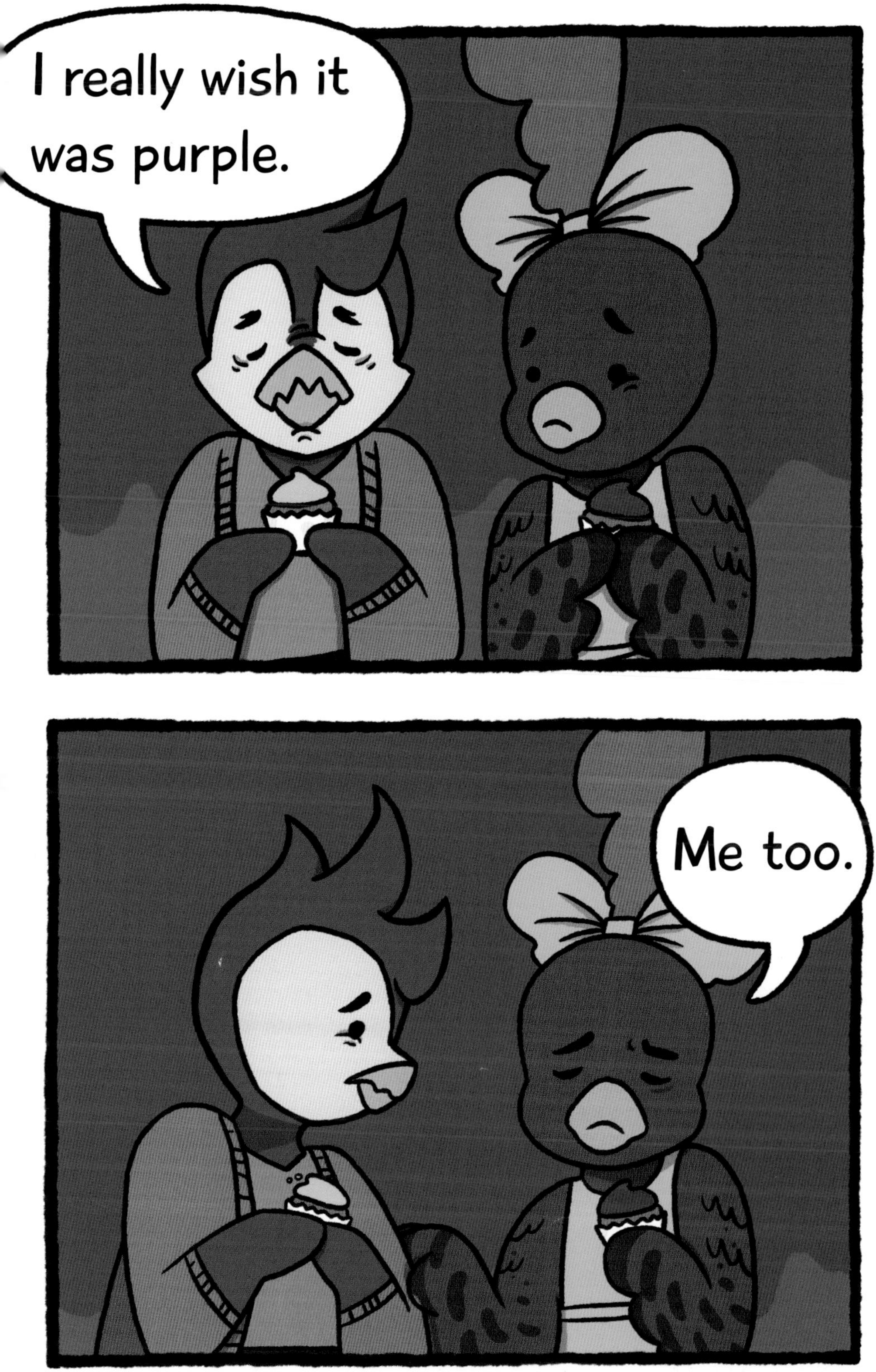
I really wish it was purple.
Me too.

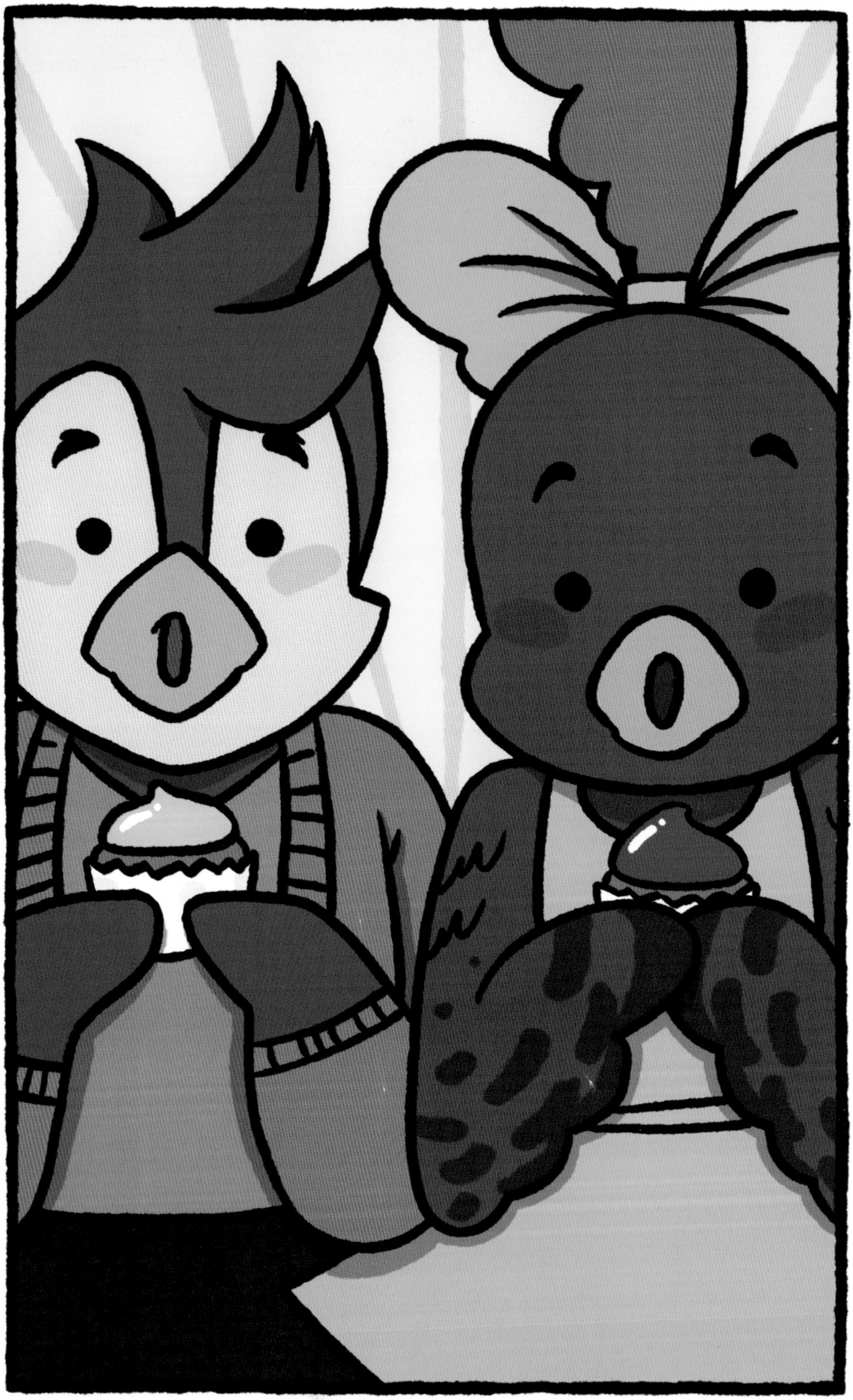

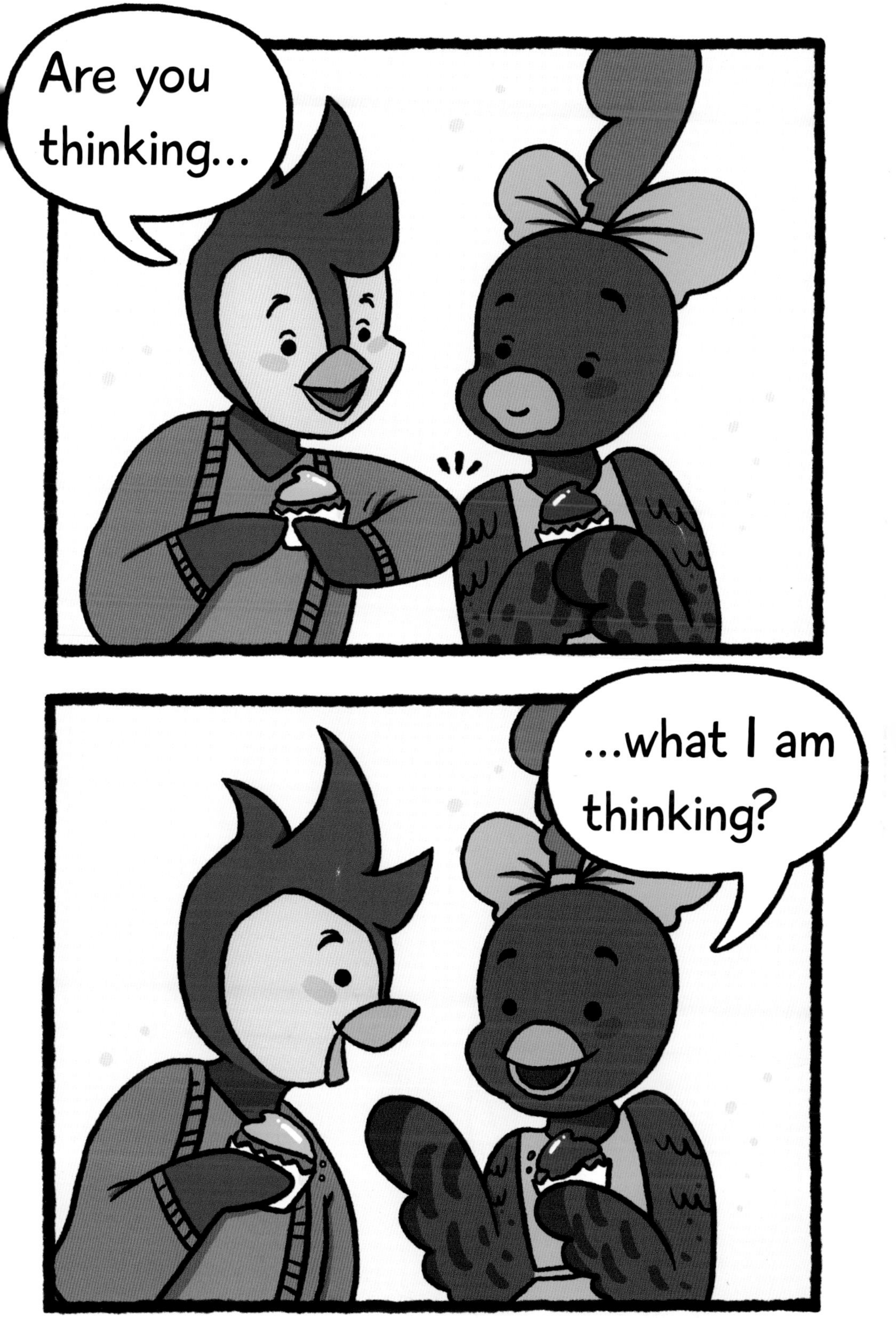
Are you thinking...
...what I am thinking?

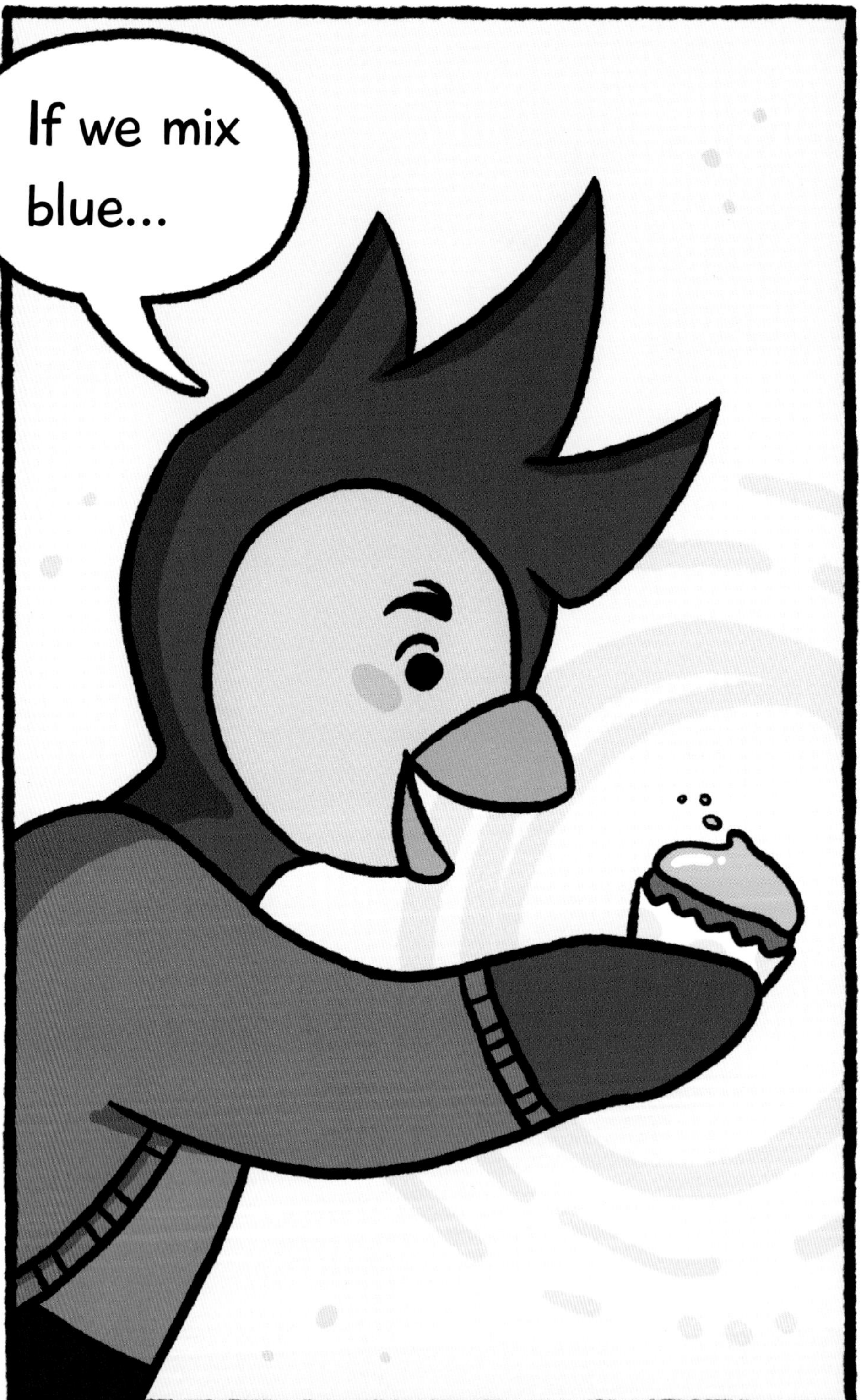
If we mix blue...

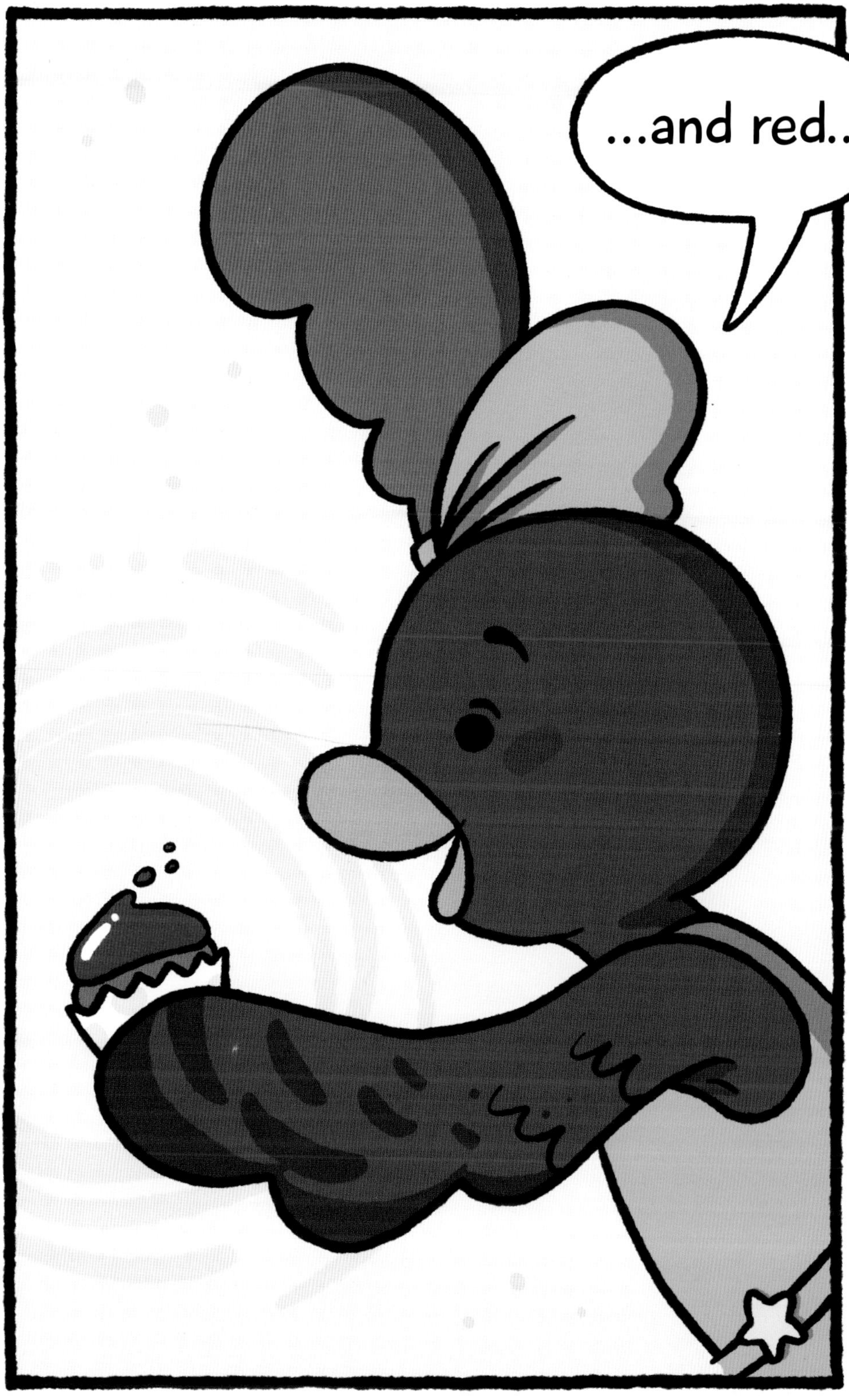
...and red...

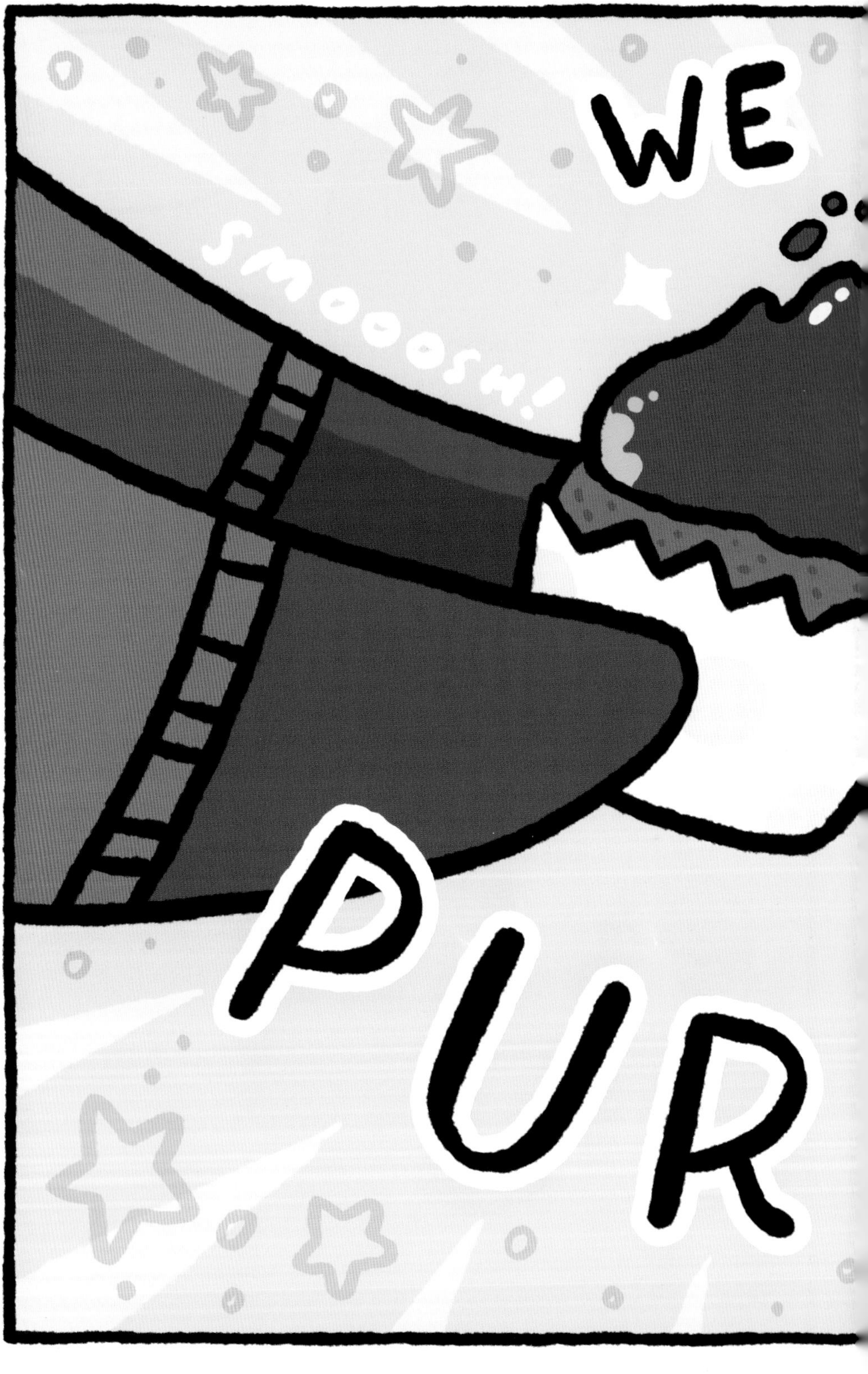
WE
SMOOOSH!
PUR

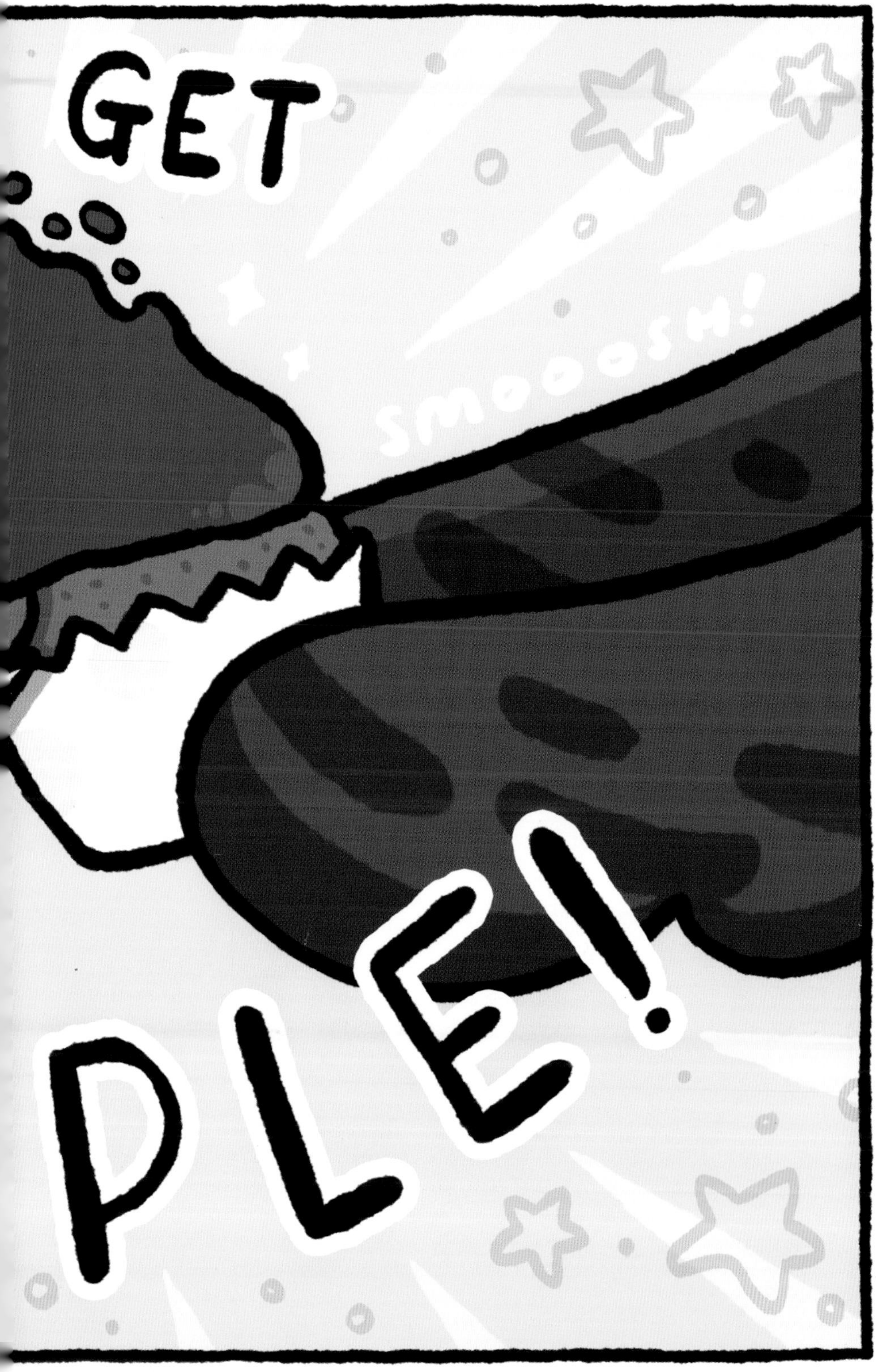
GET
SMOOOSH!
PLE!

Chi-Chi and Pey-Pey are the very best of friends. Cupcakes are delicious.

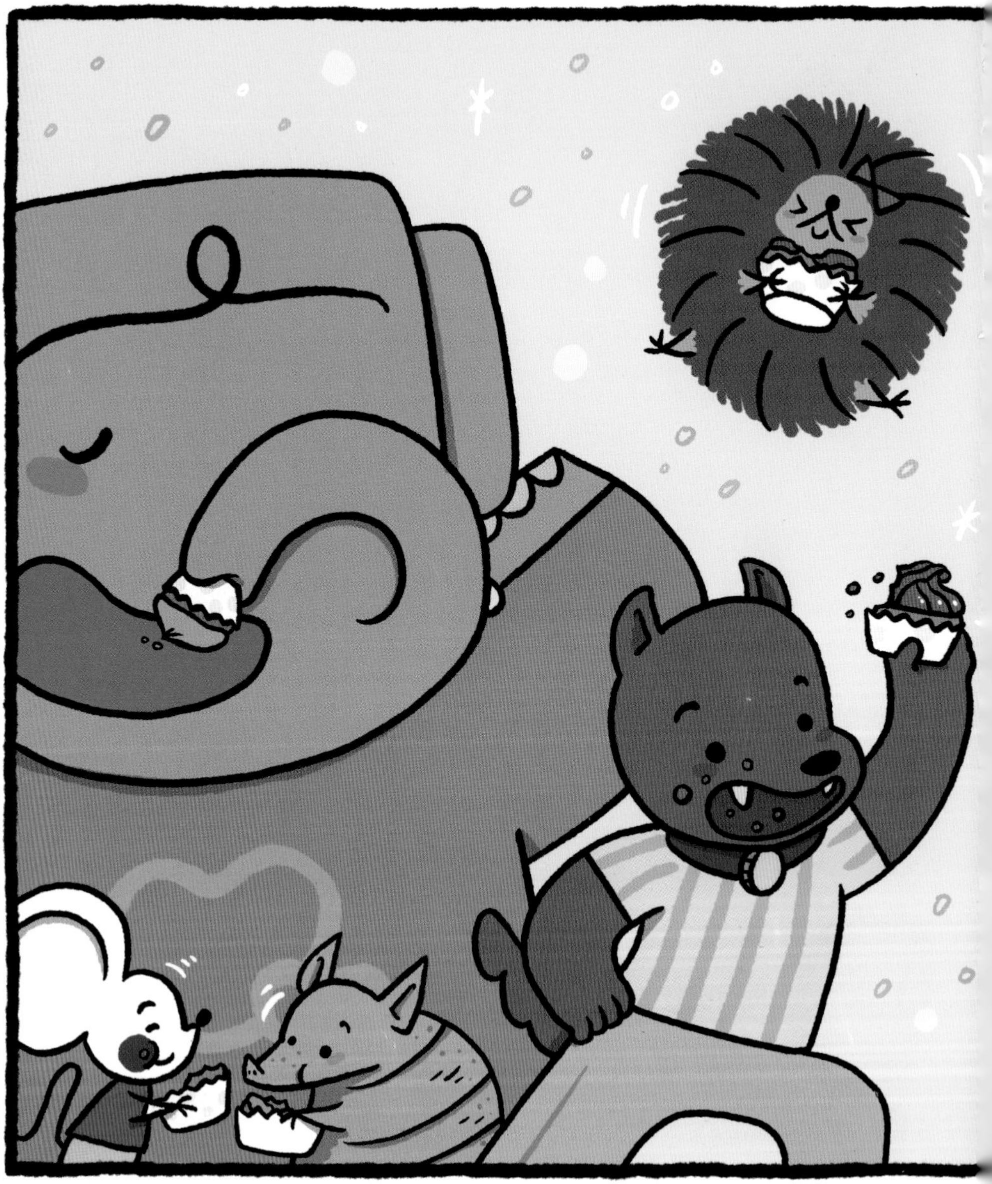

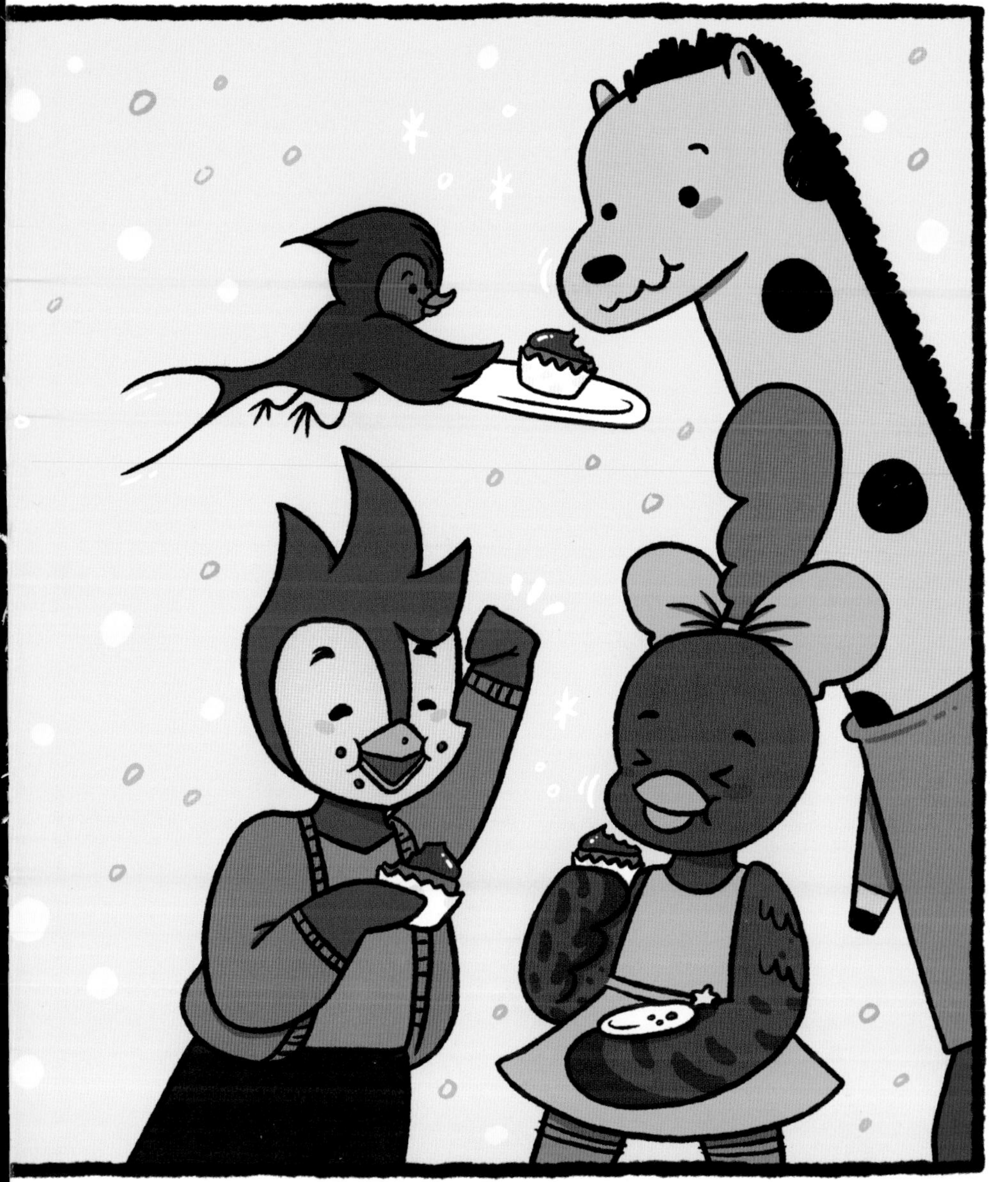

And everyone is happy.

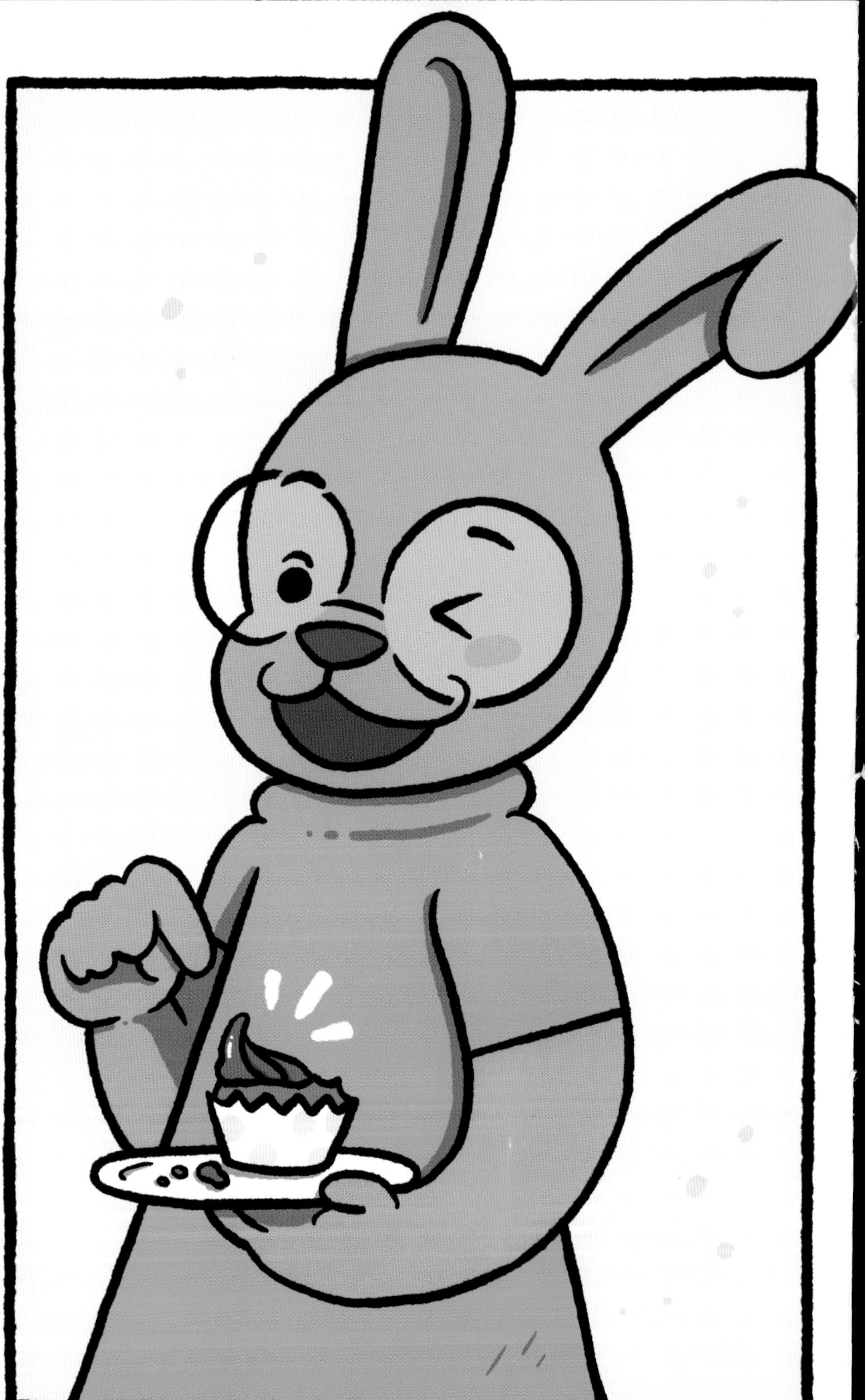